I0611390

Double-Head

BY THE SAME AUTHOR

The Perfume of Lust

Gaston Danville

Double-Head

translated, annotated and introduced by
Brian Stableford

A Black Coat Press Book

ISBN 978-1-61227-912-1. First Printing. January 2020. Published by Black Coat Press, an imprint of Hollywood Comics.com, LLC, P.O. Box 17270, Encino, CA 91416. All rights

Introduction

"Double-tête" by Gaston Danville, here translated as *Double-Head*, was first published in 35 episodes as a feuilleton serial in *L'Oeuvre* between 29 June 1927 and 9 August 1927. It was not reprinted in book form. *L'Oeuvre* was a left-wing pacifist periodical founded in 1904 by Gustave Téry, a former reporter for *Le Matin* and *Le Journal*, initially as a monthly, and then as a weekly, before becoming a daily newspaper in 1915. By 1927, it was selling over 100,000 copies.

A long gap separated the publication of "Double-tête" from Danville's earlier ventures in fiction, but it is not necessarily the case that it is entirely a product of its time. Indeed, it seems to be a patchwork that fuses together what might well have originated as three distinct stories, one being a naturalistic narrative about stock-market manipulation and the remaining two endeavors in speculative fiction, one extrapolating the notion of technologically-aided telepathy and the other detailing a quest to rediscover the alchemists "philosopher's stone" capable of transmuting other substances into gold. It is possible that the original drafts of all three stories were written some time before the publication of the hybrid, perhaps predating the Great War.

Although "Double-tête" seems to represent a deliberate attempt to move downmarket, and to produce an item of popular fiction rather than the more pretentious work that Danville had done in the early years of his career, its two components nevertheless retain an interest in the philosophical corollaries of the ideas they address, and an intense interest in the psychological peculiarities of their characters. The gap in continuity, therefore, is not as vast as it may seem at first glance, and "Double-Tête" is an interesting addendum to a career that seemed to have been abandoned more than twenty years before by one of the most intriguing dabblers in imaginative fiction to emerge during the turbulent *fin-de-siècle*.

"Gaston Danville" was the pseudonym of Armand Blocq (1870-1933), the younger brother of the neuro-physiologist Paul Blocq (1860-1896), a colleague of Jean-Martin Charcot at the Salpêtrière hospital in the late 1880s. Danville was one of the principal collaborators involved with the early issues of the *Mercure de France*, founded in 1890 by Remy de Gourmont, Alfred Vallette and others in order to provide a voice for the burgeoning Symbolist Movement. The *Mercure* was not the only periodical that attempted to do that, but it was by far the most successful, and it survived long after the movement in question had lost its crusading zeal and Symbolism had melted into the general cultural background, eventually being overtaken as a contender for the literary *avant garde* by its more exotic descendant, Surrealism.

At the time of the *Mercure*'s foundation, the Parisian literary scene was replete with disputes between various literary "schools" and "movements," of which Symbolism was one of the most prominent; it had developed out of Romanticism, once seen as revolutionary in its reaction against Classicism, but long lapsed into a kind of orthodoxy. The term "Symbolism" was closely associated, in the contexts of those disputes, with "Decadence," a label once resolutely adopted by some of the more radical Romantics, after having initially been leveled at the movement as a term of abuse by the critic Désiré Nisard, and resurrected in the 1880s as an assertive banner. Symbolism was widely seen as being engaged in a crucial rivalry with Naturalism, which was considered by many commentators to have recently evolved from its origins in the work of Émile Zola and the Goncourt brothers into a "neo-Naturalist" phase represented by "psychologists" such as Paul Bourget, who placed more emphasis on the literary examination of internal states of mind than external behavior in their accounts of the human predicament.

The apparent opposition between Symbolism and Naturalism was illusory, a phantom of publicity, and had much to do with the fact that the Symbolist school was primarily a school of poetry, crucially associated with avant-gardist poets, such as Stéphane Mallarmé and Jean Moréas, whereas Naturalism was primarily a school of prose fiction, closely associated with the evolution of the narrative techniques of the novel. Naturalist novels did not shun the employment of symbolism as a narrative device; nor did Symbolist writers, when they diversified into prose fiction, shun the naturalistic devices developed by novelists in the interests of representational verisimilitude. Leading writers of both schools shared a keen interest in the seamier side of social life, and were routinely preoccupied with erotic and violent subject-matter. Nevertheless, many of the individuals caught up in the controversy did see themselves as being involved in an ideological conflict of sorts, and were sometimes eager to take up positions in the front line, firing their critical weapons with reckless abandon. Gaston Danville was one of those, but he was exceptional in the particular stance he took, and the location from which he elected to campaign. He was, in a sense, the most ideologically-extreme of the neo-Naturalists, but he took up his position at the very heart of the Symbolist movement.

Alfred Vallette became the editor of the new *Mercure*, and his wife Marguerite, who had already become famous under the pseudonym of Rachilde, became one of its most frequent early contributors, along with Gourmont, Jules Renard and Saint-Pol Roux, all of whom would have identified themselves unhesitatingly as devoted Symbolists. To begin with, essays and reviews took up the bulk of its pages, mapping out the field of Symbolist literature and art and promoting its virtues; and while the page-count remained at its initial figure of 32, priority was given to poetry with regard to creative material. Once the number of pages had been doubled to 64 at the beginning of 1891, however, prose fiction was able to play a more important parallel role in carrying forward the ideals of the movement.

Much of the *Mercure*'s early prose fiction was very brief, in the tradition of the "prose poetry" that had been launched forty years earlier by Aloysius Bertrand and Charles Baudelaire, and subsequently hailed by Joris-Karl Huysmans as "the osmazome of literature." The fictional contributions to the magazine made in its first few years by Gourmont, Saint-Pol Roux and Renard all belonged to that lapidary tradition, and many of the other contributors followed suit, although, when Vallette was able to increase the page-count again, to 96 in 1893 and 128 in 1895, he was progressively able to find room for longer works, including serial novels—and when its periodicity eventually increased from monthly to fortnightly in 1905, those serial novels, in accordance with continuing changes in literary fashion, became a far more important feature. From the very beginning, however, Remy de Gourmont was interested in expanding the scope of pr ose-poetry be yond t he m erely l yrical, a nd adding more substance to it. In that quest, Gaston Danville must have seemed to Gourmont and Vallette to be a useful a lly; h is early c ontributions to th e m agazine r e-semble st andard exercises i n Symbolist p rose-poetry, and the series he began to develop from them, collective-ly ent itled "C ontes d'A u-Delà" [Tales o f the B eyond], seemed a n atural d evelopment i n terms of t he elabora-tion of their narrative method and thematic concerns.

Vallette w ould h ave f ound out s oon enough t hat Danville d id not c onsider himself to be a S ymbolist a t all, but he obviously did not consider that to be a reason to e xclude h im from the pe riodical, the s cope of w hich he w as pr obably a mbitious t o br oaden f rom t he v ery start—and which did, indeed, ultimately become a mag-azine of g eneral l iterary i nterest, as the S ymbolist cr u-sade in which cause i t ha d been launched i ncreasingly came to resemble a fad, and somewhat passé. At any rate, although Danville was never to appear as prolifical-ly i n the pe riodical's pages a gain a s he di d i n 189 1-92, he r emained a regular c ontributor f or m ore t han thirty years; i t se rialized two of hi s nov els an d published a good deal of his non-fiction.

In 1891-92 Danville published twelve "Contes d'Au-Delà" in the *Mercure* (tr. with other material in *The Anatomy of Love and Murder: Psychoanalytic Fan-tasies*) and added two more in 1893-4, but after that he changed di rection m arkedly. D anville's first nov el, *Les Infinis de la chair* [The Infinity of the Flesh] (1892) car-ried forward the project that he had begun in the "Contes d'Au-Delà," as he explicitly st ated in the preface to the first of them, which explained the theory behind the sto-ry series and advanced the claim that it would attempt to take t he N aturalist ca use t o a n ew bu t l ogical ex treme.

That essay also identified Symbolist and Decadent litera-ture, in contrast to the various subspecies of Naturalism, as "degenerate." The introduction is dated 1 November 1892 and is, therefore, contemporary with Max Nordau's scathing attack on *fin-de-siècle* "degeneracy," *Entartung* (1892; tr. as *Degeneration*), which Danville could not have read before offering his own thesis, although he might well have had some inkling of Nordau's argu-ment; Nordau wrote the book in Paris and had a very strong interest in contemporary psychology, so he might have been acquainted with the Blocq brothers.

Vallette evidently did not take offence at the de-scription of Symbolism as an essentially degenerate form of literature, but it probably did not endear Dan-ville to some of his fellow contributors to the *Mercure*, even those who, like Remy de Gourmont, were perfectly willing to consider the adjective "decadent" as a com-pliment. Danville's novels do not appear to have enjoyed much success, however, and such celebrity as he still retains is almost entirely based on his non-fiction book *La Psychologie de l'amour* [The Psychology of Love] (1903), which went through numerous editions and was still in print when he died. He also wrote two other non-fiction books dealing with psychological issues, *Magnétisme et spiritisme* (1908) and *Le Mystère psychique* [The Mystery of Mind] (1915). *La Psychologie de l'amour* was contemporary with Remy de Gourmont's *Physique de l'amour: Essai sur l'instinct sexuel* (tr. as *The Natural Philosophy of Love*), which was published by the *Mercure*'s press in the same year, and makes an interesting comparison with Danville's book. Danville's "Contes d'Au-Delà" were composed and published alongside some of the stories that Gour-mont subsequently collected in *Histoires magiques*

(1894; tr. in *Angels of Perversity*) and both series are illuminated by a comparison that suggests a certain mutual influence. The two authors must surely have discussed their parallel non-fiction projects, and their relevance to the fiction they were writing.

Danville's work was, of course, unable to be any more sophisticated than the prevailing ideas of its era, and it did not take long for the psychologists on whose work it is principally based—primarily Théodule Ribot,[1] of whom Paul Blocq was a dedicated disciple—to fall out of fashion.) Danville moved gradually away from those ideas in *Vers la mort* [Toward Death] (1897), *Les Reflets du miroir* [The Reflections in the Mirror] (1897), *L'Amour magicien* [Love the Magician] (1902) and *Le Parfum de volupté* (1905; tr. as *The Perfume of Lust*)[2], and that gradual disconnection from his initial purpose might well be one of the reasons why Danville did not continue writing novels after publishing *Le Parfum de volupté*, and is surely partly responsible for the different philosophy of procedure adopted in "Double-tête."

The explicit connection that Danville tried to forge between literary endeavor and psychological science had, however, been tacit since their origins and had inevitably become more obvious over time. The notion that literary depictions of human psychology, especially its

---

[1] Théodule Ribot (1839-1916) was one of the great pioneers of "positivist" psychology, explicitly based on the philosophy of Auguste Comte, which eliminated from consideration all the nonmaterial attributes associated with the "spiritualist" school, attempting instead to formulate an entirely physical notion of mentality. Unlike his brother, Danville did not agree with Ribot's stance entirely, and hardly seems to belong to the positivist school at all, although he is clearly influenced by it.

[2] Black Coat Press, ISBN 978-1-61227-580-2.

more exotic manifestations, constitute a kind of research and analysis that can and ought to be considered a kind of *avant garde* of the science, perhaps far ahead of it in sophistication, had been proposed long before the 1890s, and the argument was viable long before the advent of the novel, perhaps extending all the way back to Homer. What was original about Danville's work in that vein was not so much his literary ambition but his conviction that literature had recently lost its lead in the quest to generate understanding of human behavior and mentality, by virtue of maintaining overdue allegiance to obsolete models of motivation and the mind. Perhaps he had too much faith in the potential of contemporary psychology to correct that flaw, but he was surely not mistaken in his conviction that the literature of the future could and would benefit from a further development of its scientific sophistication, especially in the artistry of its dealing with the human Beyond of the unconscious mind. "Double-tête" lacks the literary pretentions of the author's early novels, but it does not lack his intense interest in the psychology of his characters and his determination to represent that psychology in a manner that was as unconventional as it was insightful.

When "Double-tête" was published there had been relatively few attempts in French speculative fiction to address the theme of telepathy, in spite of precedents being set in much earlier periods by such endeavors as *Le Miroir des princesses orientales* (1755; tr. as "The Enchanter's Mirror"[3]) signed "Madame Fagnan," and *Le Lorgnon* (1831 tr. as "The Lorgnon") by Delphine de

[3] Black Coat Press, ISBN 978-1-61227-820-9

Girardin.[4] "Double-tête" was published a year ahead of the first significant twentieth century *conte philosophique* to explore some of the corollaries of the notion in a sweeping fashion, *L'Homme qui lit dans les âmes* (1928; tr. as *The Man Who Could Read Minds*)[5] by Paul Gsell, and although Gsell's novel goes much further in its investigation, it is not impossible that his train of thought received some stimulation from Danville's feuilleton.

The theme of manufacturing gold had been much more widely treated in fiction, and Danville's truncated account of a problematic success stops far short of the account of technological transmutation given in Fernand Mysor's *La Ville Assassinée* (1925; tr. as *The Murdered City*)[6], but it is distinctive not only in the narrative strategy forced upon it by the confusion with a frame story but also in its representation of the awkward and theoretically challenging nature of the transmutation process. It is surely a pity that the discussion begun between the eccentric scientists who run into the acute theoretical and practical problems associated with their variant of transmutation is so abruptly short-circuited within the story in the interests of narrative convenience.

Perhaps both stories would have been more interesting had they been developed separately and each of them had been extrapolated much further, but the manner of their presentation is not without interest, and both are sufficiently innovative and sufficiently intelligent to transcend their deliberately vulgarized format. In spite of

[4] Included in *Balzac's Cane*, Black Coat Press, ISBN 978-1-61227-368-6.
[5] Black Coat Press, ISBN 978-1-61227-860-5.
[6] Black Coat Press, ISBN 978-1-61227-791-2.

being a patchwork, therefore, and the rather brutal fashion in which its two plots are brought rudely to a dismissive conclusion, the epilogue to Danville's career as writer of speculative fiction has considerable imaginative substance, and deserves to be reckoned a significant contribution to the genre.

This translation was made from the copies of the newspaper reproduced on the Bibliothèque Nationale's *gallica* website.

Brian Stableford

DOUBLE-HEAD

There are other ways to knowledge
than the habitual ways.
Professor Charles Richet[7]

I. The Wooden Spoon

The third Saturday of May 1898, in London, did not present any really special sign, even for a conscientious observer. After lunch on that day, therefore, the banal aspect of the district of Hampstead did not permit Jim Broks to foresee the series of events that the afternoon was to inaugurate, of which he was the hero and the victim, and which we shall attempt to report here.

Everything that it is permissible to say on the subject of that Saturday, so ordinary in appearance and yet so important for the person that occupies us is that the last day of the week was very different from the preceding ones, which had been dirty and damp, by virtue of a particular limpidity of the atmosphere. a crystalline blue

---

[7] Charles Richet (1850-1935) was a Nobel Prize-winning physiologist who devoted many years to the study of what would nowadays be called parapsychology. He worked for a time at the Salpêtrière with Jean-Marin Charcot, where he would certainly have met Paul Blocq, and probably his brother. He also wrote fiction, including a good deal of *roman scientifique*, mostly under the pseudonym Charles Epheyre.

sky, an almost summery temperature, and an abundance of light rather rare in that season.

Thus, when Jim Broks came to see his sister, his brother-in-law and their children, which he was accustomed to do regularly on the eve of every Sunday, he found the entire family installed in the open air.

The garden of Mansur Cottage was composed essentially of a large oval lawn circled by a gravel path, skirted to the right and left by flower beds, dominated by low brick walls, at the foot of which, in accordance with the season, forget-me-nots and daisies wilted, or begonias, geraniums and chrysanthemums. Near the villa, the principal path went past clumps of spindle-trees and aucubas, disposed symmetrically. Finally, at the other extremity of the rectangle formed by the terrain, it was subdivided into a minuscule labyrinth planted with trees of meager foliage.

At that place, beneath a clump of lilac, the master of the house, Cyrus Humber, was swinging in a rocking-chair with his arms folded over an abdomen that was already bulging, smoking a short wooden pipe with the happy tranquility of a tradesman in the City whose fur and leather business had demonstrated, for another week, the solidity appropriate to a well-known and prosperous firm. His wife, a dull and dreary creature, whose red hair redeemed by its rich tones all the poverty of the rest, was watching the games of two young boys and the baby.

The elder of the sons, Norman, was trailing his six and a half years on all fours for the moment, in the middle of the lawn, carrying the five years of little Robert on his back, while young Nelly, three years old, was trying to follow them, crawling on her belly—all, of course, accompanied by shrill cries and bursts of laughter.

As soon as Uncle Jim came in sight, Norman got up abruptly, without the slightest concern for Bob, who, after rolling in the grass, not without complaisance, collided with the baby and immediately hastened to hug her in his arms, kiss her with vivacity and recount a thousand marvels about Uncle Jim, in order to prevent a crisis of tears. The noise stopped Norman, who had already launched himself at a gallop toward the visitor, and caused him to run to help his younger brother pick Nelly up. Then the three children launched themselves forward, scolded by their mother, who enjoined them—without any great success—to show some restraint in the demonstration of their sympathy.

"Sit down, Jim. How are you?" asked Cyrus Humber of the newcomer when the latter, having favored a triple attempt to scale his person and responded to multiple compliments, kisses, and trivial chatter, was abandoned by the children. "Will you have a cigar?" he added, holding out his case.

"No, thank you," Jim replied. "I have a slight headache."

Mrs. Humber smiled at the last words.

"Oh, Mary," said her brother, "so you're still as malicious as you were in the days when you called me Double-Head, affirming that the slightest headache was bound to attain insupportable proportions in me, by reason of the development of my cranium. But I responded to you that the height of my forehead only testified to the fecundity of my intelligence."

"And you were right!" approved Cyrus, "for you're damnably clever. Old Sam Lane, who knows what's what, assured me this morning on the tube between Aldgate and Baker Street that there aren't many brokers like you on the Stock Exchange, and that you're perhaps the only one who can walk without stumbling on the accursed American paths where so many others have broken their legs."

"In saying that, Sam Lane is unjust to my associate," declared Jim, modestly. "I assure you that in this story, Judge led everything."

Cyrus Humber made a gesture of negation. "You're so adroit," he said, "that if you wanted to, you could also make us believe that. I'm not trying to insinuate that Judge...no, Judge is a good associate for you, laborious and learned...very learned...between us, I've never understood why that fellow continues learning a host of things, why he's obstinate in working on tasks foreign to his métier during entre evenings and nights, instead of resting after days that are fatiguing, nor why he takes pleasure in reading books on mathematics, medicine, philosophy, etc. etc..."

"He claims," Jim replied, "that his science had often aided him to get out of difficulty, to find the solution to questions that others would have found hard to resolve, and to foresee events that he—I ought to say we—have predicted.

Cyrus Humber was unconvinced. "You believe it," he said, "and he claims it, and I'm not as familiar with these matters as you are, nor as learned as him, but after all, in my party, I'm not considered as a fool or ignorant. I can assure you, Jim, that to appreciate the value of a good cowhide, practice is better than theory. And you won't prevent me from thinking that in your line of work it must be the same.

Mrs. Humber intervened. "Let it go, Cyrus," she said. "Don't try to convince my brother. Jim Broks and Faxton Judge aren't two associates or two friends, it's rather necessary to consider them as a small mutual admiration society. When Jim talks about Faxton, he attributes a whole lot of merits to him that Faxton keeps in reserve to unwrap as soon as it's a question of Jim. If I possessed a natural jealousy I wouldn't support without suffering the fact that Judge has acquired such a position in my brother's affection."

"Are you speaking seriously, Mary?" Jim asked.

"Very seriously," Mrs. Humber replied—which determined a crisis of hilarity in her spouse.

"In that case, my dear," he declared, puffing with laughter, "it's me who ought to be jealous of Jim!"

In truth, Jim's physique legitimated that kind of sentiment rather poorly. A brown suit dissimulated insufficiently, under the elegance of its fabric and the neatness of its cut, a slightly hollow chest, poorly muscled arms, long thin legs and a slight, gangling body, which sported in Cyrus's brother-in-law the head to which he had owed since his youth the nickname he had recalled a few moments before. The excessive thinness of a narrow face with a twisted nose, framed by cheeks that stuck exactly to prominent cheekbones, then hollowed out too rapidly, emphasized the truly prodigious height of the forehead, a pale wall commencing at the bushy eyebrows and prolonged immeasurably by the retreating curve of a vast dome, above which a thin tuft of curly pink hair floated.

That face and that cranium would have attained ugly deformity if, protected by prominent brow-ridges, in the depths of which they resembled clear fresh water, augmented by ripples, in the hollow of a double grotto, the eyes had not counterbalanced them by means of all the sympathy that their blue, intense and luminous life suggested, overcoming the unfavorable impressions that their frame procured.

For the moment, their gazes took an interest in the game of the children, who were building sand-castles in the pathway. Thus, Jim did not take up his brother-in-law's comment, but said: "Would you permit me to go and help those young architects a little?"

The "young architects" saluted the arrival of Uncle Jim with a salvo of savage cries, accompanied by an explosion of foot-stamping. Then they explained at length what they were attempting to edify; they offered to his admiration the interior disposition of the roofless castle; he was shown successively the parents' bedroom, the nursery, the bathroom, and others. It remained to establish a park, for the design of which his aid was requested.

But Nelly, who had been expressing her joy for a moment spinning round like a large blonde and pink top, abruptly let herself fall, dizzily, on the fragile walls, which collapsed; and, terrified by the immensity of the disaster, she began to sob lamentably.

Then Uncle Jim picked up a wooden spade, brandished it above his head, posed it on the summit of his cranium and sketched a smile, which suddenly ended in such a frightful grimace that the desolate Nelly, while two large tears finished rolling down her red plump cheeks, started clapping her hands and shouting: "Again"

With slow, astonished gestures, and an extraordinarily grave face, which amused the baby and her brothers greatly, Uncle Jim obeyed.

When he removed his improvised headgear, to their great joy, the children saw him inspect the surroundings in the fashion of someone trying to discover the author of a disobliging joke, turn the spade over in his hands, contemplating it with a kind of curious alarm, and caress

it sev eral t imes, all while manifesting an extreme su r-
prise. One cou ld have sw orn that i t w as the f irst time
Uncle Jim ha d be en a uthorized t o look c losely a t a nd
touch s uch an object. He c onsidered i t a t l ength, han-
dling it l ike r are porcelain, or a v aluable a rchaeological
find. H e d id no t w eary o f e xamining, s ometimes t he
short handle, sometimes the moderately hollowed spoon,
the v arnish of w hich, cracked in places di splayed the
fibers of vulgar wood, scratched by the ridges of stones,
soiled by earth and detached in places.

Suddenly, the a musing man ceased his pantomime
in or der t o c ommence a nother, i n w hich the w ooden
spoon, which he threw away, no longer figured.

Slowly, he g ot up, t urned his he ad a nd shook i t in
the manner used to discourage an annoying insect. Finally, he sat down on the edge of the lawn and lent a excessive a ttention to t he di sorderly bounds by m eans of
which Norman, B ob a nd Nelly w ere t estifying a g aiety
that w as not w eakening. He folded hi s a rms a nd c losed
his eyes, equally di sdainful of t he f light of swallows i n
the sunlit sky and t he joyful expressions of the noisy
trio, gesticulating nearby on the pathway.

Meanwhile, Cyrus Humber, who was stuffing a new
pipe, declared to his wife: "Your brother is truly remarkable, Mary. I could never amuse the children as much as
him."

That sincere admiration displeased Jim Broks' sister, who, too artful to allow her intimate di scontentment
to be di vined, was ne vertheless una ble to constrain herself t o e nthusiasm, a nd onl y pe rceived t hat i t w as tea
time.

She communicated that ob servation to he r brother,
at a d istance, by m eans of s hrill m odulations t hat
brought t he y oung man t o hi s f eet so a bruptly t hat t he

children applauded and Bob asked his elder brother in a low voice: "Isn't Uncle Jim a clown?"

In that word, Bob placed a world of superstition, and he pronounced it with a slightly fearful respect, which that sort of person inspired in him. He venerated clowns as the equal of mythological and supernatural beings, and he was not far off believing that it would be easy for them to accomplish feats of which he often dreamed, such as flying through the air to pick cherries from the tree, and then eating them head down with his feet hanging on to a cloud, or some other estimable fantasy forbidden to mere mortals.

Norman knew the value attributed by Robert to the magic word and, being deprived of critical intelligence, had never thought of diminishing it. He reflected momentarily that Uncle Jim seemed to him to be sufficiently worthy to merit the glorious name. By virtue of a residual scruple, however, he admitted to Bob that he did not know.

While the caravan was heading toward the house, for the garden furniture had not yet come out of storage and it was not yet convenient to take tea in the open air, Jim Broks, following his sister and his brother-in-law, muttered between his teeth: "Dirty kids! What does all that signify? Devil take them with their damn toys! I don't understand it at all. Only Judge can get me out of this!"

That did not prevent him, however, from making kisses as resonant as slaps reverberate on the cheeks of Nelly, Bob and Norman at the foot of the staircase, where the little band separated from the parents in order to go up to the nursery, nor from responding amiably to the compliments that Cyrus Humber lavished on him regarding his practical knowledge of the art of amusing children.

Before penetrating into the dining room, Jim spotted the telephone apparatus placed in a corner of the hall and excusing himself in order to use it. He turned the handle and as soon as the bell rang he demanded: "Central 255!"

Mary, who had heard him through the door, which stood ajar, closed it and said to her husband: "He's telephoning Judge.

To which Cyrus Humber replied, very sagely: "That's quite natural, my love."

As soon as he was alone and had obtained the connection, Jim spoke in such a fashion that his words could not be heard distinctly in the next room.

"Hello! Yes, it's me! I absolutely must see you, Faxton, the sooner the better... No, it's not a matter of Stock Exchange business... No, it's not a family matter either... nor a private matter. No, it's something else... Well, the thing is... it's terribly difficult to explain, especially over the telephone... Serious? To the point that I think I'll go mad if you don't intervene... Really...! I repeat, it's impossible for me to give you the slightest useful indication... When...? This evening! Thank you! You don't know how much pleasure it gives me to hear you speak, and over the wire... You can't know...a thousand thanks! Understood, this evening...!"

Afterwards, it was at a brisk pace that Jim Broks went to rejoin his brother-in-law and his sister. He was whistling a tune from an fashionable operetta when he installed himself in his favorite armchair, near the bay window, which caused Cyrus Humber to say: "How's your headache?"

"Oh, it's passing, thanks," said Jim. "A cup of tea or two and..."

"An evening at t he t heater w ith Judge," a dded Mary.

"Precisely, an evening with Judge," Jim confirmed, smiling, "and this accursed headache will, I hope, have quit m y doubl e he ad. A l ittle m ore cream, pl ease, my little Mary."

II. An Absurd Story

The cab carrying Jim Broks sped alongside the rails that carried intermittent little red trams, and then plunged northwards into the heart of a horribly muddy district. People in haste to finish their shopping on Saturday, since she shops would be closed on Sunday, were tramping in a badly-dressed swarm, which overflowed the sidewalks to the middle of the causeway in spite of the width of the streets, continually at risk of being run over, placidly allowing themselves to be splashed and persistently hampering the progress of the vehicle, to the despair of the driver, who was forced to execute prodigies of skill.

Jim Broks, slumped on the back seat, did not hear the curses of his driver, nor the hubbub of the crowd, any more than he discerned the shifting silhouettes outlined against the bright shop-windows, incessantly renewed. Various thoughts preoccupied him, all related to the same incident. Had he not been wrong to telephone Judge? Should he not have kept the absurd story secret? Perhaps it was only a malaise due to the excessively hot sun, a fugitive hallucination, a vertigo caused by an imprudence...perhaps, after having crouched down for a long time playing with his nephews he had stood up too precipitately...

How was he going to explain to Judge that stupid adventure, unworthy of a serious man? And what would his associate say? What if he advised him to consult a doctor? If he were prescribed a treatment, a long rest, what would become of the business? Judge didn't know

25

the c lientele as w ell as h e di d; he k new t he A merican market by heart, but as for the rest...

Jim thought that he had not yet reimbursed the lesser pa rt of the p artnership t hat h ad be en g enerously a dvanced to him three years before, without informing anyone, almost secretly, by old Sam Lane, confident in the young man's star and desirous of having an agent at the Exchange devoted to him, who could favor certain speculations on s hares t hat the f inancier s ponsored. I n the calculations the two of t hem ha d made, v acations a nd illness were not foreseen.

Jim's ang uish increased to the p oint t hat h e w as tempted to tell the driver to turn round...

The ho rse w as now trotting r apidly a long t he m iddle o f a de serted avenue bordered by g ardens and l ow houses. Jim s ighed; he w as t wenty m eters from J udge's dwelling.

As Mary's brother m ade a principle of following the indications of ha zard, which he called destiny, he accepted to descend from the vehicle, and to accomplish the or dinary r ites of a rguing a bout the pr ice of the journey w ith the c abby be fore pa ying hi m a nd r inging the bell of a door framed by a balustrade with white pillars.

He f ollowed a y oung maid c oiffed w ith a lace butterfly. Smiling, after having rid him of his hat, cane and cloak, she led him to the far end of the ha ll, to her master's study.

Faxton Judge, c omfortably seated i n a large l ow armchair upho lstered in dark red morocco, was a waiting Jim's v isit next to a bright coa l fire, rereading a v olume of Spencer.

Electric lamps, simply suspended by braided wires, veiled by t ransparent bells w ith c rystal f ringes, illuminated a room furnished with a sober luxury found in the slightest details, from the old Delft vases setting above the long lemonwood book cases the symmetrical pallor of their tapering roundness, to the modern objects on the shelf-units of the mantelpiece and the unsilvered mirror protecting the marquetry of the desk, a marvelous eighteenth-century table.

As soon as his associate was introduced, Judge dismissed the maidservant and authorized her not to wait up. Then, taking him to a side-table where there were carafes of fresh water, goblets, ice-buckets trimmed with silver next to bottles of soda and old Danish flagons containing various alcoholic beverages he asked: "The usual, Jim? Lots of soda and a splash of whisky?"

"If you like," replied the young man, mechanically.

"By the way," said Judge, who produced the mixture offered, "What you said on the telephone this afternoon, apart from the indication of your visit this evening, really wasn't very clear. I was very intrigued by that gibberish, but I believe I might have guessed what it's about."

"Really? That would be surprising," said Jim.

"Not as much as you suppose," said Judge, "for after you left the office this morning, Lane rang and I responded in your stead. Tell me, Jim, in complete confidence, are you certain that the old boy isn't bluffing with this Peruvian Nitrate? You remember his Venezuelan affair..."

"It's not the same thing at all. How can you compare them? Come on! A month ago I brought his private engineer to dinner, who was about to return out there. You know that he explained to us what he'd seen and what he intended to do. There's no bluff in that enterprise, I swear to you. The proof is that we're letting the price fall."

"That's it! That's exactly where it's spoiled. The shares are already lower than they need to be, and it wouldn't take much, if they fall any further, for the bearers of obligations—and the Lawsons, who you were wrong to let in on it—to protest, and even demand a liquidation."

"Evidently, I suspect that if the affair is ruined, they'll doubtless take it up on their own."

"Well, the old man told me this morning that he's learned that your former director, that rogue Wirsea, to whom you gave a good chunk of shares in the Syndicate, is trying to exchange them, now that they're exchangeable, for cash. Suppose those shares fall into a market that's already depressed and that Lawsons also decide to sell theirs…there'd be a complete collapse."

"Bah! Since he hasn't released any yet, it's because he isn't ready to let them go so quickly."

"Thus far, yes, probably because he's too wily. I think he'd like it to be the Lawsons who strike the blow, so that he, Wirsea, while obtaining the same holding and the place of director in the new company, will make a profit on the sale of his shares, which he can do on the smallest rise in prices. If you really have confidence that the affair is worth as much as Sam Lane thinks, one could try to profit from the hesitation that's holding Wirsea back, and even roll him over in his own villainy—but it won't be easy, since he wants to sell relatively dear, and who will buy them? Sam Lane is stuffed with his Peruvian Nitrate, and we…as for the clients, it's pointless to think about it."

"Oh…as for Wirsea, I'll take charge of making him lower his prices. The first thing is to make sure of the Lawsons. You say that we were wrong to bring them in, but in reality, they wouldn't take the risk of picking up a demolished affair, and Wirsea is mistaken on their account. They're not men of his species, and they have information on his account too solid to act, as he imagined, on his indications alone. Once the Lawsons are fortified, we'll see what Wirsea has in his head. Perhaps he's only acting out of an urgent need for money. I've known him for a long time...and if he needs money, we have him. In any case, I'll go to see Lane at home tomorrow."

Jim Broks emptied his glass and lit a cigar. Professional concerns had lightened the anguish that had almost made him turn back in the cab. He was no longer thinking about anything but Peruvian Nitrate and its principal shareholders. So he started in annoyance when Judge asked him: "Isn't that what was preoccupying you so much this afternoon? Doubtless Lane telephoned you at home?"

"No, not at all," he replied.

"Well," said Judge, "in that case, give me the key to the enigma, for I observe that I've played the role of Oedipus very poorly. I've thought successively of Wirsea and Co., some mischief of your sister Mary, or that they want to marry you off. It's something else, then?"

"Something else entirely," said Jim, with a sigh, and added, as Judge got ready to mix a new drink: "Would you like, by virtue of a special violation of my habit, to increase the dose of whisky...considerably, for once. Yes...a lot of whisky and a dash of soda."

His associate looked at him in astonishment.

Jim laughed bitterly.

"Oh, Faxton, you're not at the end of your surprises. What I desire to confide to you will appear even more improbable than my present request. In fact, there's only one man in the world to whom I'd dare to relate it, and that's you. But I beg you, in the course of our conversation, he re a nd now, ha ve you noticed anything…suspect…bizarre…extravagant…let's say t he word: a nything *insane*, i n m y s peech? R espond t o me frankly."

"I c onfess t o y ou, Jim, t hat I don' t und erstand t he meaning of that question."

Judge's associate made a slight movement of impatience. "Don't t hink s o much, F axton," he s aid. "It's a matter o f t elling m e s quarely w hether, in judging t he Wirsea-Lawson a ffair, m y mind a ppears t o y ou t o be enjoying a complete lucidity, its habitual equilibrium."

"Certainly. I can affirm that you've appreciated the situation like a man in possession of sound judgment."

"One m ore qu estion. I s i t pos sible that I …that a person…can apparently act in the same fashion as an entirely he althy pe rson, i n t he o rdinary a ction of life, before the people who know him best, without them suspecting anything abnormal, but in spite of that possess a seed of m adness…very s mall…for example, strange sensations, hallucinations of a sort?"

"An i nvalid of this s ort c an e vidently di ssimulate sometimes, but h e can 't al ways di ssimulate, indefinitely."

"Ah! *They* dissimulate! They hide their… hallucinations eh?"

"It's v ery di fficult for m e, Jim, to g ive y ou a complete l ecture on the m atter, a ll the m ore s o a s no thing authorizes m e to think tha t it w ould be of t he s lightest use to you, for if we go on like this we risk talking without und erstanding ne another: y ou a bout something t hat clearly interests y ou, even preoccupies y ou; me a bout vague, indeterminate, general phenomena probably irrelevant to your particular case. Nevertheless, on the matter of ha llucinations a nd d ementia, I 'll t ry t o i nform you briefly, a lthough I de test anything r esembling popu lar lectures a nd o ther a ttempts a t popu larization. S o, w hat constitutes m ania or d elirium i sn't so much the h alluci-nation as its interpretation. Do you understand?"

"Not very well."

"I'll give you an example. Admit for a moment that you or I suddenly feel a pain in the side. Probably, we'd limit o urselves to r egistering the fact w ithout c ommen-tary, a s l ong a s the pa inful s ensation w asn't pr olonged, unless we attributed i t t o ne uralgia or r heumatism. An invalid of the kind to which you've made allusion would interpret the sensation in an a bnormal f ashion; he 'd in-voke oc cult influences, hidden e nemies, de mons, e lec-tricity…in brief, construct a system of ext raordinary ex-planations."

"You're r ight, F axton. I t's be tter if I t ell y ou m y case simply, for I can't see any more clearly than before. On the c ontrary! I thought, in fact, that I must be going mad, s ince I'd experienced s omething resembling a hal-lucination. H owever, de sirous of not judging m yself t o be ill, I formed the hypothesis that it was a matter, not of a ha llucination, but o f s omething e lse, on w hich o ne could i ndeed con struct a system of ext raordinary expla-nations. It m ight be that in seeking a cure I've aggravat-ed my situation. That's it, isn't it?"

"What do you want? I don't know, myself."

Well, Faxton, I know that you've overturned all my plans, and now I f ear *interpretation*. That's what you call this k ind of de mentia, i sn't it? I nterpretation? S o, I repeat, I'll tell you everything. It's preferable that I pro-ceed without further ado with the story of the event, and then you can *interpret* it at your ease, without my fearing madness."

Judge started laughing. " My poor Jim," he said. "What a singular fear! Has whatever has happened to you this morning terrified you that much?"

Before replying, Jim Broks rummaged in the inside pocket of his jacket and brought out his portfolio. He took out a few papers, on which Judge recognized his friend's delicate and regular handwriting.

"It's more serious than you imagine," he said. "It happened this morning at Mansur Cottage. I drafted a few notes when I returned home. This is it! I was in the garden with the children; my sister and brother-in-law were some distance away. For some reason, I can't remember why, little Nelly started to cry. In order to console her, or distract her, I took it into my head to pick up a spade that was lying on the ground and put it on my head. Then..."

"Pardon me," Judge interrupted. "What do you man, exactly, in taking about a spade as headgear? You put a spade on your head? But a spade as flat..."

"Not that kind of spade," Jim relied. "The one I'm talking about was a child's toy; it's one of those shovels that affect the form of a wooden spoon, or, more precisely, a small soup-ladle, and, in consequence, a hollow object of which, once the concave part was applied to the top of my head, the convex part simulated a sort of ridiculous skull-cap."

"Ah! Right, I see. Go on, I beg you."

"Alas, my dear friend, as soon as I had done that. I immediately fell into an unusual state of mind, rather difficult to describe. Without transition, without any preliminary vertigo, without a second of malaise or slight daze, I was instantaneously *doubled*, if you'll permit me that expression. In any case, it remains inexact, imperfect and approximate. Any yet, understand by the term that from that moment on, Jim Broks became Jim Broks *plus someone else*, who was added, a second individual who doubled him—and that will be accurate!

"Understand me well: I continued to see the garden lawn with *my* eyes, my ordinary eyes, the ones that are looking at you now, my Jim Broks eyes. I could still distinguish Mansur Cottage, the open g round-floor windows, allowing me—I remember this detail—to discern the form of the grand piano, a few items of furniture, fake art-works and plants that my sister likes to pile up on the drawing room sideboards, tables and mantelpiece. I heard with *my* ears the laughter of the children, the sound of their footsteps on the gravel path. In brief, I hadn't ceased to take account of the environment I was in.

"But, doubling that familiar décor without effacing it, a different place was superimposed on it. I saw with *second* eyes—there's no other way to translate my thought—I saw, confusedly, an enclosed space…at least, I knew that it was closed, that it had to be a room, because I divined, rather than perceiving clearly, a piece of carpet, such as one encounters in furnished apartments, which was only revealed as a red patch limited by a black patch—a table—another black patch—doubtless the corner of a fireplace—and nothing else...

"In reality, it isn't by deduction that I've arrived at calling the red patch a carpet, the place a room, and the black patches a table and the corner of a fireplace. No! I was conscious of the nature of those objects, in a fashion as certain and as vivid as the one that permits me at present to recognize the form of the poker with which you're stirring the fire, although, nevertheless, my second eyes were functioning rather poorly. At the same time, my second ears were disagreeably impressed by the very special grating that a pen produces in drawing cross-hatching on paper. I didn't know yet who was writing...

"That hallucination—that's what I called that horrible doubling—only lasted a few seconds. It stopped—retain this detail well—as soon as I had taken the spade, the wooden spoon, off my head..."

"Hmm!" said Judge. "How were you so clearly informed that the place where the red patch and the black patches were must be a room? How did you divine immediately, since your second eyes were informing you imperfectly, that it was a matter of an enclosed space?"

"Because *I was there!*" replied Jim Broks, with vivacity. "I was sitting in that room and I recognized a piece of *my* carpet, *my* table and *my* fireplace!"

"Did you also recognize yourself?"

"What?"

"You've talked about a doubling. You've also declared that you were in your room. I'm asking you in what form your *double* appeared to you, and in what fashion you recognized yourself in the seated person."

"A double? No, no! There was no one there who resembled me: neither the man who was writing, nor the other..."

"What other?"

"Yes! I forgot to tell you that I knew that another individual... at least, I think that another individual was in the room... I had a sort of presentiment of it. The second time, I had the proof that I wasn't mistaken."

"Wait, please," implored Judge, extending his right arm. "Don't go so fast, because this whole story is still terribly confused at present."

"For me," Jim relied, "it was terrible clear, far too clear!"

"Hmm!" said Judge. "I can't easily see how a red patch and two black patches... that was it, wasn't it...?"

"Yes!"

"Interposed... in fact, was it through those patches that your sister's drawing room appeared, or above, or below, or... otherwise?"

"I repeat to you, Judge, that I perceived both at the same time, as if, during that short period, I possessed two pairs of eyes and two pairs of ears. Hang on—you'll understand admirably. Try to imagine the scene that a compartment of a tube train presents to you, with its passengers and its guard, while you continue looking at your table and the objects on it. Well, it's almost in that manner that the two heterogeneous spectacles coexisted, but with the difference that by intuition—at least, I supposed so—I knew where I was, although the place was only revealed to me via confused patches."

"Good, good," said Judge. "You've plugged the gaps, completed and imagined what was lacking and straightened out what wasn't straight, almost as one straightens out a phantom of a dream, a residue of a dream, a residue of a dream that persists on awakening, incoherent, disconnected and fragmentary. And, in fact, in the same fashion that you accept in the course of a dream, sometimes with complete complaisance or only slight surprise, playing the role of a child sitting on a bench in a classroom, at the same time as that of a fully-grown man devoting himself to his affairs, moving in the habitual fame of his occupations, in the state in which you found yourself simultaneously in a bizarre furnished room and in your sister's garden, you were doubtless shocked by the self-contradiction afterwards?"

"That's right, Judge," Jim confirmed. "That's what it was—a dream! A dream that continued, but awake. I believe you've found the right explanation."

He smiled broadly. "Curious!" he continued. "I'm sure now that I'm no longer ill...what am I saying?...sure that I've never been ill. A dream. Naturally: a dream. eh? One exaggerates immediately; one forges fears; one torments oneself with frightful suppositions instead of remaining calm, cool, and reasoning like you... A dream! Why didn't I think of that? It often happens that one dozes off for an instant, a second, almost without perceiving it, or without perceiving it at all. It was very hot, too, under the sun's rays, an eminently favorable condition. And then, one doesn't suspect that one has been asleep during that brief moment, inappreciable but sufficient for dreaming...and the dream continuing...a dream! It's obvious. I knew, Judge, that you'd be able to get me out of the embarrassment. Thank you, my dear..."

"Hmm!" said Jim Broks' associate. "What about the second time?"

"Ah! The second time...? The dream continued, the same dream, but less confused, for you see..."

He handed Judge a piece of paper, chosen from among the notes he had taken out of his portfolio.

"I was able to remember enough to reproduce here what I was writing out there, on the paper in the room."

Faxton read aloud:

"'...They warm themselves in winter with stones, which they dispose around their hearths and which burn...' Is that really what you were writing?"

"Yes," Jim replied.

"But this is written in French," said his associate.

36

"Obviously," Jim replied, without the slightest embarrassment, "it's a translation; a sort of exercise, or something of the sort."

"What are you saying? A translation! God damn me if I know of any English author who has ever been crazy enough to write about people using stones for anything but building their houses or maintaining the roads. Disposing stones in a hearth would signify, I suppose, building a chimney, not hoping to obtain a means of heating from the stones themselves. No one, I think has emitted such an absurdity. I know that, rigorously, one could obtain sparks by striking flints...all the same, Jim, try that method for burning pebbles! How can you warm yourself in winter with stones?"

At that final question, Jim Broks became excessively cheerful. Disorderly laughter shook him all over, to such a extent that his face became congested, and it became impossible for him to utter a word for some time, except for onomatopoeias, utilizing all the vowels in the alphabet in turn, accompanied by convulsive gestures."

As soon as he had calmed down, he said: "Ha ha! Truly, Faxton, my dear friend, you don't understand. Ho ho! Truly...look, then, Faxton, look at your own grate in your own fireplace. Don't you make use of stones, pray? Of black stones? And in our country, isn't that combustible material used quite generally? Warm oneself with stones! How, Faxton, can one warm oneself with stones! Ha ha ha!"

Jim Broks' hilarity resumed its abnormal course.

Judge, meanwhile, was not laughing. He was considering the note that his associate had handed him and rereading quietly the phrase written in French.

"Hmm!" he said, then. "Other words exist in English or in French to designate that. Why have you chosen *pierre* rather than *houille*, or coal?"

"Me?" cried Jim. "What are you saying? Was it me? I've already told you that there was no one there resembling me."

"Pardon me," Judge objected. "You also affirmed: *me, I* was writing in that room...*I* knew that it was *my* room and its carpet, *my* fireplace..."

"Oh, I beg you, Faxton, don't complicate this absurd dream story. You explained everything very well just now. Don't rack your brains any more on that subject."

"In that case," Jim's associate persisted, "you truly don't know the reason that led you...led the man in the room...the man who was sitting in the room, writing, if you prefer...to write *pierre* rather than putting *houille*, or coal?"

"Yes," replied Jim, absent-mindedly, and speaking automatically, "I repeat that it's a translation...a translation of an old traveler's tale, almost a legend...a local legend...that I was translating into French as an exercise..."

At those words, the placid Judge bounded out of his armchair and, taking his associate by the shoulders, shook him violently.

"Come on!" he cried, exasperated. "Is it really you, Jim Broks, born, I think, in Newcastle, in the midst of coal-mines and mountains of coal, who is pronouncing such words? A traveler's tale! A local legend!"

"Why are you getting carried away?" said Jim, tranquilly. "Have I said anything stupid? It was in my dream, this...in my dream, don't forget...! Hang on! I remember now...the other man, the one who was looking over my shoulder...what a diabolical face he had! It seems to me now that I knew that face...but what's the matter, Faxton? Why are you widening your eyes like a frightened chicken? Yes, the first time, I only knew that there was someone in the room. The second time that individual—I have his name on the tip of my tongue: Drummel, Strummel, Dormell... it's extraordinary! You know, I'm sure that I know him... in sum... Romnell, assuming that Romnell is his name, but it wasn't exactly Romnell... got up to see what I was writing. And can you imagine that that damned Romnell asked me the same question as you? He too asked me why I'd written the word *pierre*? Now I remember very clearly that I made that response: a traveler's tale, a sort of legend..."

"But from what country? Where do people not know the use of coal?" Judge asked.

"Yes that's right! In what country?"

Jim Broks remained thoughtful. Then, after a brief moment of recollection, he allowed to escape, in a sing-song manner, unexpected modulations that surprised Judge.

"The Japanese, in that epoch, only knew wood and charcoal. The traveler was surprised to see stones burning...black stones..." Immediately afterwards, it was in his ordinary voice that Jim asked: "Well, what do you think, Judge?" Immediately afterwards, he added: "What does it matter? It was a dream. There are always extraordinary inventions in dreams. One imagines the worst stupidities. If we were to leave that stupid adventure and talk about more interesting things, my dear Faxton, that would be better."

Judge reflected for a few moments, and said: "You didn't think of keeping the wooden spoon, the spade?"

"Of course not. What would I do with that toy?"

"That's unfortunate. You should have brought it to me."

"Seriously? I should have...but for what..."

Judge interrupted him, and began a sentence that he did not finish: "Don't you realize that if you'd taken the precaution of keeping the spade, perhaps..."

He shook his head without continuing, until Jim questioned him.

"What connection does that spade have with the legend...and my dream? I think the sun had a more important influence, and also the reflection of the sunlight from the sand of the pathway..."

"In sum," Judge articulated, with difficulty, "is the idea repellent to you of trying...of attempting a sort of reconstruction of the scene? I'd like to try that experiment. I believe that there must be utensils in the kitchen analogies in form to that wooden spoon. Will you lend yourself to that trial? It's necessary to place an object of that sort on your head, exactly as you did this afternoon."

Jim Broks smiled. "Oh, I'll accept gladly," he declared. "Very gladly, as long as I'll only have you as a witness of that ridiculous action. Your cook..."

"Don't worry. She must have gone to bed at the same time as the chambermaid. Well?"

Instead of getting up, Jim Broks slapped the arm of his chair violently with the palm of his open hand, and remained seated.

"In truth, Judge," he said, "I'm very sorry that I told you about that idiotic dream. Now you've been seized in your turn, as I was, by an obsession, by the folly of interpretation. Natural, simple, ordinary causes are no longer sufficient for you. You want to experiment. The wooden spoon has to serve as a magical instrument for gathering de mons, for c ollecting w andering s pirits a nd pouring them energetically through the skull. You doubtless w ant t o t ry t o e voke di sincarnate s ouls by t hat means! Be careful, my de ar F axton. You're interpreting terribly, and what c onstitutes delirium is t he interpretation, isn't it? Remember what you told me about that!"

"You're mad, Jim."

"Oho! Don't pronounce that word lightly! It sounds very di sagreeably on my eardrum. I don' t be lieve I 'm already m ad, but I ha ve a di abolical fear that y ou o r I might g o mad w ith t his da mned s tory of a w aking dream. A nd i t w ouldn't be a g od t ime, da mn i t, f or Wirsea would then have a clear field to demolish Peruvian Nitrate and the Lawsons, to bring down Old Lane and bury his reputation under his great affair. He'd die of it, poor old Sam!

"Come on, F axton, think about y our ne ighbor and abandon this fantasy. Wait until our railway is constructed all th e w ay to th e c oast, our installations concluded and we ha ve st ocks i n reserve...and Peruvian Nitrate is quoted a t t en pound s. T hen, I'll p ermit y ou t o e xperiment as much as you like and to employ me in your trials, if it amuses you."

At that gibe, Judge could not suppress a smile. "Hmm!" he sai d. "Do you believe t hat P eruvian Nitrate will ever be quoted at ten pounds?"

"My ol d F axton, y ou're talking lik e a client, or Lawson junior, but y ou're amusing me greatly a nyway. So, no m ore w ooden s poon, or dr eams! It's unde rstood that I 'll go to s ee o ld S am t omorrow, a nd, s ave for extreme ur gency, w hich I don' t foresee, w e won't see one another ag ain until M onday. F orgive me or ha ving d e- prived y ou of t he theater this e vening a nd ha ving t old you these extravagances. I was so anxious, but I'm absolutely relieved. No need to ask you the secret, even with old Lane, eh? Anyway, from now on I'll mistrust the sun's rays, my nephews and...wooden spoons. What am I saying? You're going to ask me to experiment..."

"No, Jim. Not this evening."

"Ah! I can breathe! By the way, seriously, aren't you going to advise me to take up a vegetarian diet, or to abstain from some beverage...tea, alcohol...?"

"I'm not a physician, my dear Jim. In any case, I don't believe you've arrived in the realm of the pathological in the slightest."

"So much the better, Faxton, so much the better! Firstly, because 'pathological' is a frightful word, and secondly...I don't much like diets. Good night, old chap. A thousand thanks, again...and, until Monday!"

III. Cyrus' Victory

Situated on the third floor of the Saint Barnaby Building, one of the enormous edifices that have been replacing for several years in the City of London a block of houses destroyed by fire, in imitation of American skyscrapers, the name of which they have borrowed, possessed of almost as much importance but not the height, the private office of Broks and Judge obtained light from a large courtyard via panes of frosted glass, opposite which a door gave access to the corridor that served all the offices on that floor. It was placed between two other rooms of unequal size: one, the larger, accommodated the employees, and a part of it, separated from the rest by a partition, was destined for the admission of clients; the other, the smaller, was reserved for brokers' agents, telephone booths and automatic apparatus for transmitting information from telegraphic agencies. Its furniture only consisted of the indispensable: two varnished mahogany desks, devoid of style, over-burdened with stacks of paper and cluttered with various models of telephone; a few armchairs, a safe, a cupboard serving as a wardrobe; and a filing cabinet. The walls displayed mining diagrams and maps. A marble fireplace sheltered a small coal fire.

It was Monday morning.

Jim Broks had just come in, and, after having exchanged a few banal words with Judge, without either of them making any allusion to their conversation of Saturday evening, he sat down at his desk.

Half a hour went by without a word being pronounced other than in reply to an employee or a correspondent.

The two associates opened their mail, continually disturbed either by knocks on the door to the right, preceding the entrance of a boy bringing documents to be signed or by the ringing of bells necessitating brief telephone conversations. Both of them were habituated to those continua interruptions, however, they did not trouble the mental lucidity of the placid Judge or the activity of Double-Head, who, unhooking the receiver for the sixth time, tipped his chair back and started rocking while opening and closing the drawer situated to his left.

That familiar tic always indicated in him the presence of a certain ill humor. After a minute of hesitation he decided to express it.

"Another order to sell Peruvian," he said, "from Cushing, and at any price. Decidedly, they're mad..."

"Hold on, Jim," replied Faxton Judge. "Here's a piece of paper from Maddock that will give you pleasure."

He held out a letter.

"No thanks," said Double-Head. "I know that Maddock has Peruvians...and where do these damned imbeciles want us to find buyers? Anyway"—he took out his watch—"I have to go see the Lawsons."

"Good," said Judge. "Wait a minute, for it's important that we're in accord. I think that Lawson junior will drop Wirsea's name, invoke Wirsea's information, and even, if Lawson senior doesn't stop him, go as far as talking about liquidation. At that moment, you know what you have to say about our good friend Wirsea, without forgetting to mention that he's in Paris at the moment, in the process of arranging a copper deal, in which he has a personal interest, hence his intention of selling his Peruvian shares—for, as you suppose, it's to procure money that he wants to cede his entitlements. I'm informed; Wirsea doesn't have as much importance as the Lawsons.

"For them, by way of conclusion, you can communicate confidentially the cablegram that old Lane gave you yesterday, announcing the placement of the last meter of rail, the beginning of trials of the track, and allowing the anticipation that our first loads will be expedited to Europe within a month. Then they'll be the buyers of all they want to sell at present, for in spite of your good opinion on their account, Jim, have no doubt that although they were sent by Owen, Cushing, Maddock and others, this morning's orders bear the signature Lawson.

"We'll take advantage of it, moreover, to establish prices as low as possible before they adopt another attitude; it's necessary not to forget the worthy Wirsea, and that lesson will also teach the Lawsons not to try to play tricks on us. Now, you can go!"

Jim Broks had stopped manipulating the drawer. He looked at his associate with admiration.

"Decidedly, Judge," he declared, "You're marvelous."

"Afterwards, Jim!" replied the latter, smiling. "You can compliment me afterwards, when you get back—with these people, nothing is certain."

Someone knocked on the door to the corridor.

"Come in!" he said.

It was Cyrus Humber who was introduced, and who immediately headed toward his brother-in-law, holding out his hand. But the latter, who had already closed the door of the wardrobe, from which he had rapidly extracted his overcoat, cane and hat, showed some rudeness in his welcome.

"Sorry, my dear Cyrus," he said. "Very little time at the moment. I hope that nothing disastrous motivates your visit. No? All your little society well, my sister too? Then…you have something to say to me?"

"Yes," said Cyrus. "I desire your advice for a placement; I presently possess…"

"Oh, my dear, you know that we limit ourselves here to carrying out orders. We sell and we buy because people ask us to sell or to buy. The client has his opinion formed. Furthermore, I have a principle, which you know: I don't do business with my family. Go to your bank; they'll give you excellent advice. As for me, apart from never influencing a client, I never—I repeat, never—do business with a relative. It's pointless to insist. In any case, I must run…a meeting! Excuse me."

And Jim Broks left precipitately, leaving the excellent Cyrus collapsed in an armchair.

Nevertheless, the merchant of fur and leather pulled himself together quite rapidly. He put down his umbrella and top hat, which he had kept thus far in his hand, like a man who intends to affirm that he is not to be put off so easily. Then, taking a cigar-case out of his pocket, he held it out to Judge.

"Thank you," said the latter, "but I don't smoke."

"That's all right," said Cyrus, choosing a Havana, which he lit carefully. My…brother-in-law…is a trifle abrupt…don't you think?"

"Come on, my dear Mr. Humber, you know what business is. Would you have liked it any better if he had missed his meeting in order to chat with you?"

"Chat! Chat!" rectified the fat man. "Pardon me! I've come here as a client. This, in sum, is what it concerns..."

"Hmm!" said Judge. "I regret to interrupt you, but after what Jim has told you, you'll understand how delicate it would be for me to listen to you. I'd give the impression of disapproving of my associate's conduct, and that I can't do; I truly can't. Furthermore, I'm here on my own. I still have a heap of letters to open, orders to execute...I must beg you to be indulgent."

"Evidently," observed Cyrus, "given that my brother-in-law...however, there might be a means of reaching an understanding, all the same; I'd like so much..."

"Be reasonable, my dear Mr. Humber. I assure you that it's infinitely disagreeable for me to have to disoblige you, and I'd be equally in despair in appearing impolite toward you..."

"Oh, I'm a tradesman, aren't I? And I know..."

"Well, if you absolutely desire to speak to Jim, will you accept to have lunch with us at the Throgmorton?"[8]

"That's a good idea, Mr. Judge. I consent willingly. However, I'll make one condition...I'll pay for the lunch."

"So be it. You're not a client."

Cyrus Humber laughed loudly "Not yet!" he rectified. "Not yet...but I will be!" He stood up and added: "Since it's agreed, I'll run away. You're busy; I won't disturb you."

After the departure of Jim's brother-in-law, Faxton Judge expedited his affairs rapidly, more by means of

---

[8] This is a slight anachronism; the famous Throgmorton Restaurant, situated between the Bank of England and the Stock Exchange did not open until October 1900.

professional automatism than the consciousness that he usually brought to the execution of his quotidian labor.

His staff made topical remarks about the attitude of the boss—who had not responded personally to a telephone call from the Gibsons of Edinburgh, although he normally demanded that communication with those gentlemen was reserved for him, even if he was on the floor of the Exchange—in which Wirsea and Peruvian Nitrate occupied a large place.

At the Stock Exchange, Judge barely responded to the salutations of the liveried ushers charged with forbidding the profane access to the temple, exchanged distracted handshakes, abridged conversations in low voices with the agents, and appeared so visibly estranged from the noisy life of the groups that a quarter of a hour after his arrival the most regrettable rumors were born about Peruvian Nitrate, immediately welcomed, and passed on, magnifying rapidly and translated into a drop in shares bearing the name of the unfortunate Society from an opening price of thirteen shillings, already judged weak, to nine.

An hour later, the drop accelerated swiftly, and there were no longer any buyers at four.

In the office of Broks and Judge, the telephone bells were making such a racket that Judge ended up no longer answering them, even to old Sam Lane.

In truth, in spite of the gravity of the situation, Faxton was scarcely thinking about Peruvian Nitrate, nor about Sam Lane, Wirsea, Lawson and the others. If he had succeeded in dissimulating the veritable direction of his thoughts from his associate and Cyrus Humber, he had only obtained that result at the price of an energetic mental tension. After that the haunting had recommenced, the obsession with the absurd story that Jim had told him the other evening.

He had retained the most insignificant and the most ridiculous details of it, to the point that the scene was reconstituted of its own accord in his thoughts, almost as clearly as if he had witnessed it. And it irritated him not to be able to reduce the elements of it to known principles, for the explanations he had given to Jim, which Jim had adopted with enthusiasm, had never satisfied him.

All of Sunday, which he normally devoted to sport or mundane duties, Judge had spent searching his library, to the great despair of his housekeeper, who had previously admired her master's regular habits. His research had been prolonged far into the night. The result of that for Judge was a kind of mental curvature, so to speak, aggravating his physical fatigue.

He had not, in fact, in the course of his long excursion through his books, encountered any of those definitions that are as restful as a comfortable chair, or any of the typical examples with which he would have been able to proceed to a convincing confrontation, which might have furnished the troubling case with its identity, denomination and civil estate. Departing from the disturbances of hysteria and hallucinations, he had crossed the frontier, sometimes indecisive, that separates nervous disorders from mental illnesses, without finding either in one or the other a territory where it would have been legitimate to assign a domicile to the phenomena confessed by Jim.

What was the significance of that consciousness of two simultaneous and different lives, in two milieux, one real and the other imaginary, but imposing itself with the authority of the real? A duplication of the personality of that sort, involving the coexistence not merely of two different mentalities but of two dissimilar environments, had never been observed.

How could propositions as contradictory as "I was writing; I recognized my room," and "There was no one resembling me sitting at that table," be explained? In what fashion, too, could the singular phrase "They burn stones in their hearths," be interpreted, and above all, the promptitude with which Jim had found that phrase quite natural, and the response which he had furnished almost immediately: "In that epoch, the Japanese only knew wood and charcoal. The traveler"—what traveler?—"was surprised to see stones burning, black stones."

In front of the fireplace, above which were displayed, pinned to the wall, the designs of excavators destined for the exploitation of Peruvian Nitrate, Judge, deaf to the carillon of bells and indifferent to the noise of conversations that were being exchanged in the neighboring rooms, the serious, placid, intelligent Judge, surprised himself repeating the bizarre phrase in a low voice, while gazing at the ashes and the blackened coke that filled the grate, where the fire was extinct.

Suddenly, he cried out: "But what if it were true! After all, it isn't absurd!"

The sound of his own voice surprised him unpleasantly.

"Damn!" he said. "I'm talking aloud now!"

But that only continued for a moment and his thought continued to follow the same path.

Yes, he reflected, *the use of coal has become familiar to us, but it isn't ridiculous to suppose that an individual, an absolute stranger to that particularity of our civilization, might have been surprised to see rocks of a sort, minerals extracted from the ground, susceptible of producing flames and energetic heat. On reflection, the traveler's astonishment—why Japanese, though?— seems justified. But where the devil did Double-Head dig up that story?*

Hmm, perhaps in a conversation...something he read that he forgot subsequently...and yet, one doesn't easily forget such phrases. Perhaps, too, an anecdote of that sort was recounted near him, without him paying any great attention to it, occupied as he was with something else, and, having registered it almost or entirely unconsciously, it then required, in order for it to appear to his consciousness, some commotion, such as a commencement of sunstroke, or a benign congestion.

I believe at present that I'm on the right track and that the case is less complicated than it seemed to be at first. In sum, I've allowed myself to be drawn into applying an exceptional character to that unusual assemblage of vocables, "They warm themselves with stones," quite unnecessarily. I believe that it only intrigued me because I'd be en quite astonished by what I judged to be nonsense. In sum, I lacked coolness and logic; I've wasted my time at a moment when truly, I had better things to do...

The chain of reflections inspired in Faxton Judge by the sight of a few fragments of coke was broken at that moment by the insistence that a closed fist put into hammering at the door to the corridor. Jim's associate cut short all deduction and went to open it.

The hand that had knocked with that joyful tenacity belonged to a big, blond clean-shaven fellow, cheered up by a broad smile and with bright turquoise eyes.

"Rimney!" said Judge. "How are you, old man?"

"Very well, thanks."

"And how it it that you've disembarked in London without any warning, without a word?"

"I wrote to you, my dear Judge," the newcomer replied, laughing, "but I doubtless forgot to post the letter, for I found it in my jacket pocket a quarter of an hour ago. I'm not joking—here it is!"

"Always the same, Rimney!" Judge observed, taking the envelope. "If you consent," he added, balancing the letter between his fingers instead of unsealing it, "it will certainly be simpler if you inform me of the contents of this, which must be: 'I'll come to see you at the end of May in London…'"

"There's something else," Rimney rectified. "I announced to you that I'd quit my job as an English teacher in Paris and that I was returning to England."

"As an English teacher?"

"Exactly, and also of French."

"And you have pupils lined up?"

"It was them that begged me to change places. I traveled to London in their company. But you must be in the midst of working, to have let me wait for so long on the threshold of your sanctuary, and I wouldn't want to disturb you, given that I'm here for the rest of the year. Transmit my amities to dear Jim, unless I encounter him in the street beforehand. His activity can't have diminished, since, naturally, I don't see him in his office."

Judge had taken his watch out of his fob pocket.

"Listen Rimney," he said, after having darted a glance at the dial, "will you be kind to Jim, who'll be very happy to see you again? He'll be here very shortly, so stay and keep me company for a few minutes—all right?"

"Yes. I've nothing better to do, if I'm not inconveniencing you."

"Not at all," said Judge. "Excuse me." He was about to go into the room where his employees were, but as he w ent ou t, Rimney cal led him ba ck. "Alas!" he cried, "I'll a lways be a br ainless i diot, a nd s tupid Rimney. My pupils are waiting for me by the murals in the Royal Exchange."

"So? They can wait a little longer."

"No—really, I only escaped to come and shake your hand; but we have an entire pr ogram, and these Japanese..."

"Ah! They're Japanese, your pupils?"

"But h aven't I w ritten t o tell y ou that?" relied Romney. "It's true," he went on, laughing, "that you ha- ven't opened my letter Yes, they're Japanese, who have asked m e t o pi lot t hem t o L ondon w hile c ontinuing t o give them my lessons."

"Hmm! Japanese," repeated Judge, who was think- ing about the famous phrase. "Then you'll doubtless be in a pos ition to g ive m e s ome i nformation, w hich I 've been incapable of procuring unt il now. Is t here mention in some book from out there of a traveler who, exploring the Occident, is surprised by the sight of a coal fire...or, rather, I'm expressing myself poorly..."

"You're sure," R imney i nterrupted, "that it's pr int- ed somewhere?"

"I assume so," replied Judge.

"Well, that's curious," said R imney. "Quite recent- ly, in fact, one of my pupils assured me that there was a sort of oral legend on that subject."

"Hmm!"

"Yes. I ask ed him to write me a l ittle com position on t he impressions of a Japanese v isiting E urope—a French exercise...."

"French?"

"Didn't I te ll y ou that I 'm te aching E nglish and French?"

"That's true! And he expressed his astonishment in seeing a fireplace where coal was burning?"

"No. At first he had a curious fashion of depicting our cities and describing our aliments. Wine, I remember, evoked for him the color of blood. It appeared that among them, sake is a colorless liquid that is drunk hot. As for coal, that's very funny. He employed an expression of which neither you nor I would ever have thought; he wrote that people burned stones. Stones! Isn't that bizarre?"

"Very strange indeed And it's very recent, you say, this… narration."

"I believe so: last Saturday."

"In the afternoon?"

"Some time after lunch."

"Hmm. Are you certain?"

"Absolutely."

"That's frightening."

"What do you find frightening in that, Judge? It's rather comical."

"What?"

"Well, you've just replied to me: 'That's frightening,' and I asked you what, in your view, is frightening about it."

"Oh, not hing, not hing, my dear Rimney. I was thinking that what's frightening is the way that time's passing, and..."

"Sapristi! That's true; I must fly. I'll come back one of these days for Jim. *Au revoir*, Judge."

And the big fellow went out at a run.

Left alone, Faxton Judge shook his head in the fashion of a wet dog, and then growled in a low voice: "Japanese… an exercise written in French; it all fits. That Romnell, the face that Jim knew without being able to find the exact name, is evidently Rimney. Oh, I ought to have asked him whether he has a red carpet in his room. Then, truly, Jim was able to see that at a distance, by means of a wooden spoon? That would be terrifying!

"Let's see! Let's not go mad! After all, couldn't Jim have known by some other means, as I supposed at first, the story including the burning stones, and couldn't the association of that story with the narration of Rimney's pupil be purely fortuitous?

"No, no and no! It would be too extraordinary, even more extravagant as a coincidence, if it were such a simple co incidence. The remembrance of an anecdote couldn't have stimulated the description of those precise individuals: the man who was writing and the other, especially of Rimney, the awkward restitution of that meager décor rather than that of a club, a restaurant or a garden or some other. My version of this morning doesn't fit with the French exercise written by a Japanese on Saturday after lunch.

"Hmm...why so much doubt?

"It must be ...no, it's certainly a case—oh, t he first—the first case, surely, of true telepathy, the telepathy that a host of dramatic tales in which ridicule often carries into the marvelous, a miscellany of fantastic stories of mysterious apparitions and phantoms, described and presented in the fashion of scientific observations, has rendered inadmissible for any individual provided with an average dose of common sense. Those spectral burlesques and naïve farewell visits rendered by touching moribund individuals to their relatives and friends before the final voyage...telepathic hallucinations? Never! Pure hallucination!"

"But this, yes, it's acceptable: a sudden communication of thoughts, or, rather, an irruption, an avalanche, an invasion of strange, unknown waves, of perceptions, images and sensations superimposed on the real milieu: inexplicable hallucinations, telepathic, these!

"Evidently, if our brain can, at a given moment, cease exceptionally to be carefully isolated, as it's necessary for its good functioning that such a delicate apparatus has to be, and it then becomes susceptible to find itself temporarily accessible to vibrations emanating from other lobes than its own, it isn't absurd to suppose that those vibrations might sooner originate from relatives or friends, emerging from resonators tuned in union with our mental apparatus, a great number of ideas being common in that case. And, in fact, the presence of Rimney would confirm to a certain point that way of seeing.

"However, the childish vision of ghosts remains impossible to conceive, for we sense confusedly that we live because we think, we act, we receive multiple impressions, but without perceiving them clearly, at every moment of our existence and in the absence of a mirror, such as we appear to others.

"Thus, the apparent contradiction of Jim's words translates a reality: the Japanese, who was writing next to Rimney, whose interior life Double-Head lived for a few seconds, couldn't send back an image of himself. He couldn't see himself at that moment; his mind was impressed by other images than his own. That's the unique reason why Jim had so much difficulty when he tried to describe his "dream" in a mixed-up, difficult and obscure story, which constantly ran into pseudo-incoherences, since poor Double-Head remained impotent to give a description of the person who was writing, even though he affirmed: 'I was sitting at my table, in my room, etc...'"

Judge smiled, pensively.

"Hmm," he murmured. " The first c ase, in t ruth! Perhaps the only one? I had sensed that immediately, when I asked Jim to repeat the experiment. Fortunately, he's only opened up to me regarding the adventure, less tragic a nd m ore be wildering t han t he s upposed a pparitions of be loved individuals. He w ould doub tless ha ve been thought to be mad, and rapidly interned. Our business, in that case..."

Judge went into the room where the employees were stationed and gave his instructions for the expedition of c urrent tasks. A happy agitation had replaced in him t he pr evious de jection. H e ha d f ound h is f ooting again on the s olid g round of r eason and in life, with a sentiment of intense joy, an impression of mental lucidity such that no task seemed difficult or of-putting to him, no problem complicated.

Jim B roks ca me ba ck at t hat m oment, his exp res-sion discouraged. When he was alone i n their private office he said: "The L awsons a ren't c onvinced. I t hink the news of the completion of the line was taken by them as a s imple bl uff. All I was able to obtain after an hour of e fforts i s t hat they'll w ait for t hree da ys fo r official confirmation, w hich w ill l eave t hem t heir f reedom of action, since w e still ha ve ni ne da ys be fore se ttlement day."

"They've really promised not to sell any thing be-fore three days?"

"Yes. All the same, they've admitted that they'd be risking too much, if, by chance—I'm using their terms—Sam Lane isn't bluffing."

"Well, that's absolutely what we need."

"You're no t v ery de manding. It w ould ha ve b een better to obtain, as you hoped yourself, not only that they won't sell, but that they'll buy. Only they claimed that old Sam had already played the trick of the cablegram from his private engineer..."

"But that wasn't Ross," Judge put in, "Bridgeman, the other, had cerebral anemia; he had even deceived his colleagues with his reports. That doesn't signify anything with regard to the good faith of old Lane..."

"My dear Judge, it isn't me that it's necessary to convince. What you're telling me, I've objected in vain to the Lawsons, to such a extent that, before their attitude, I'm beginning to fear that you might be right, that it was a mistake to interest them so much in the affair, and that they're capable, if the opportunity presents itself, of demolishing it in order to take it over on their own account. And yet, if that were the case, it seems to me that they'd proceed more squarely... In any case, if the director of Peruvian Nitrate doesn't confirm in three days what I told them, they'll let go of what they still have and take advantage of the panic to provoke the dissolution of the Company in the name of the shareholders."

"Hmm! Why don't they cable at their own expense?"

"I proposed that to them; they don't want to spend another penny in this affair."

"That's unfortunate for them, excellent for us," decided Judge, coldly. "Tell Sam Lane to cable the director at Callao immediately, in order to be sure of having an official declaration before the deadline. Three days is more than we need to reckon with Wirsea. Then take the first fast train to the continent, after having asked Wirsea by telephone for a meeting, and come back here with his packet, which won't cost us much, given the present lowering of the price. You'll play the card of the dissolution of the Company demanded by the Lawsons. As he doesn't know about Sam Lane's cablegram, he'll prefer to sell you his paper for two shillings a share—he'll still make a profit at that price—than risk not being able to obtain two pence."

"Very well!" said Jim Broks. "Only, I looked in passing to see who the present purchasers are of almost all the Peruvian Nitrate sold this morning: they're the excellent Stanford, dear old Lowdes and Rose, Willy Rose in person—which is to say, Sam Lane and us. Now, he and we must be very close to the limit of our available credit, and…Wirsea needs ready cash."

"Hmm!" replied Judge. "Don't worry about those details. Stamford, Lowdes and Rose have nine days before the liquidation; they'll probably come out of it with a profit. As for the ready cash, we'll find as much of it as we need at lunch. Haven't I told you that your brother-in-law is treating us at the Throgmorton?"

"Cyrus Humber?"

"Why not?"

"What about my great principle? Don't do business with the family!"

"It's me who'll negotiate; I'm neither his relative nor his ally, I suppose. You'll consent, as a special favor, to set aside your principles for once. It will, in any case, only be a semi-derogation."

"If he knows that it's a matter of a share that has just fallen to four shillings, he won't want to."

"We'll see. In any case, it's almost time to go to the restaurant to meet your brother-in-law, and it's a matter of not keeping the worthy fellow waiting for too long. You'll soon be informed."

"Permit me to telephone am Lane first, and Wirsea, if it doesn't take too long to obtain Paris."

"Perfect. I'll go on ahead."

Judge left the office whistling an operetta tune and climbed up to the next floor, where he found a vast bathroom. While he proceeded automatically with a summary toilette, in front of an attendant eager to pass him a towel, which he used in abundance, Jim's associate deliberated rapidly: should he communicate to Jim his great discovery, the real origin of his "dream," or, since Jim had retained since the other evening a tranquilizing faith in that explanation, was it not preferable to leave him in that mental disposition, appropriate to conserve the calm that he would surely need in the circumstances?

It was the latter decision to which Judge rallied, estimating that, in order to deal with Wirsea and bring that delicate operation to a conclusion, his collaborator had no need of enlightenment regarding his own case.

Nevertheless, as he went down in the elevator, an irritating temptation surged forth in his mind: might it not be possible subsequently to utilize Jim's marvelous faculty of obtaining a voyage through brains harboring interesting secrets? To know what a Lane or the Lawsons were really thinking! To take an inventory of the secret chambers that every human being possesses, and which no one but himself ever penetrates—not even his dearest friend or passionately beloved wife! An apparatus for capturing idea, images, sensations…a machine of telepathic communication! On what principle? The wooden spoon, perfected from the viewpoint of practical application.

The wooden spoon!

At that moment, Judge crossed the threshold of the Saint Barnaby Building, and that idea, profoundly attractive a minute before, suddenly appeared to him to be merely burlesque. Seen through the damp mist that enveloped the busy passers-by in the street, cluttering the sidewalks, the immediate reality contrasted too much with that dream. He exchanged tips of his hat with colleagues and smiled.

After the liquidation, there would be time to study that question; in the meantime, it was necessary to think first about the worthy Cyrus Humber, whose capital had been offered with such a good grace that it would be ill-mannered to refuse it...and Wirsea, who would surely be even happier than Cyrus with such a victory!

IV. No. 8 La Pascalieri
No. 9 The Hakamura Family

While two black lackeys in zinzolin coats and pow-dered wigs came t o fix the number 8 in large frames placed to either side of the stage, a murmur rose up, cov-ering momentarily the fanfares of t he orchestra, and the various movements by which impatience, c uriosity, de-sire and joy are expressed, and agitated the elegant pub-lic filling th e m usic ha ll. Then everyone fell s ilent. A hundred pairs of opera-glasses aimed their crystal lenses as the faces i n t he c rowd as soon as t he v alets di sap-peared and the yellow plush curtains parted silently.

Wirsea, l eaning on t he edge of a box, p assed the program to his neighbor, Jim Broks, underlining for him with h is i ndex finger t he argument of the p antomime, above which a cartouche put in prominence the name of the principal interpreter. He w hispered: "A dmirable! Marvelous! I saw her a year ago in Vienna; it was a suc-cess!"

After ha ving t hanked h im, J im B roks pr etended t o be absorbed in the translation of the text that had been submitted to him while the figurants invaded the stage, without the financier t aking a ccount of it, for the w ord "success" evoked too many recent and agreeable memo-ries in his mind.

Success: the lunch i n t he T hrogmorton restaurant, where several subterranean floors remained the domain of men of finance, and where the only skirts perceptible usually be longed t o t he H indu c ooks, i n na tional c os-tume, who pr esided before t he pub lic i n t he con fection of a famous curry. After long efforts, Cyrus Humber had obtained, thanks to the intervention of Judge, conciliating and benevolent, that Jim would set aside his excessively rigorous principle, allow himself to yield, and consent to accept the capital fruitlessly offered that morning, to employ it for the best, without the affectation of a definitive placement.

Success in Paris, the negotiations with Wirsea! Entirely absorbed by his present copper affair, needing money in order to interest himself in it personally, he had scarcely discussed Jim's proposals, accepted the after a semblance of bargaining, and confessing, after having ceded the package of Peruvian Nitrate shares that remained to him, that he had never accorded the Lawsons the same faith that he possessed in regard to Sam Lane. He had added that in his opinion, the Lawsons were wrong to want to demolish Peruvian Nitrate, because it would fall on its own, given that there would never be anything for which to hope before a long lapse of time. He would have preferred them to help the shares to rise, or only to maintain them, but since it was going otherwise, he would be glad to get out with a small profit

Jim Broks had inferred from this speech the Wirsea did not know whether he had been sent by Sam Lane and was dealing with that money, or whether he ought to be considered as a messenger of the Lawsons. In doubt, foreseeing a struggle, in the course of which the shares might drop further, especially if the holders of obligations gambled on the threat of dissolution, the engineer, enticed by the profit of his own affair, which he considered more solid than Peruvian Nitrate, had deserted the ship in peril without further delay. Seeing him in that excellent disposition, Jim had refrained carefully from informing him or contradicting hm. He had accepted his advice like a man for whom such words remained indifferent, if not superfluous, and had applied himself to reinforcing in Wirsea the opinion that he, Jim Broks, was only playing the role of a simple intermediary, an agent sufficiently rewarded by his brokerage commission, to whom the future of Peruvian Nitrate was as unimportant as its intrinsic value.

At five o' clock in the afternoon, he had escaped from the Palace hall to telephone Judge. It was then too late to catch the London train, so he had accepted to spend the evening in Paris.

Success! It was a success!

A sound of applause, reverberating from the stalls to the boxes like hailstones on a tin roof, brought him back to the concerns of the present moment.

On the stage, the figurants finished arranging themselves in two excessively symmetrical semicircles. The décor had changed.

Jim Broks' reflections had distracted him to the point that he was surprised not to recognize the picturesque and cluttered street over which the curtain had risen, but to encounter in its place a room in a palace, in which veiled dancers, eunuchs, dignitaries and guards seemed very preoccupied with allowing the sight, in the center, of a staircase of a few steps, ending in a bay draped with long curtains, which rose slowly, over an energetic blast from the brass section of the orchestra, while La Pascalieri advanced, to the acclamations of the public, very stiff in the sumptuous costume of a Byzantine Empress, armored with gems and helmed in gold.

A light veil lent her face an immaterial softness and enveloped her supple body, but without extinguishing the gleam of her eyes or the flame of her mouth, nor the fire of the precious stones or the luster of their living case.

On seeing her, one forgot the poverty of the décor, the poor hero in pretentious frippery, amassed there for her glory, the story of the celebrated jewels constellating her breast, and the anecdote told about the chanteuse herself. Everything disappeared in a common admiration and a unanimous enthusiasm.

She removed the frail fabric, unmasking the oval of the incomparable face; thus Helen of Sparta must have appeared to the old Trojans. She was the one who, from century to century, reminds hum ans of their physical nobility and informs them that beauty sometimes lives elsewhere than the curves of sculptors, the canvases of painters, the verses of poets and the harmonies of musicians.

The crowd, even the most frivolous and the most stupid members, accepted such lessons. More than that; it received them with surprising respect. The impression produced on Jim Broks habitually occupied with professional questions, apart from the strange incident of which he had been the victim, was all the more violent because, a moment before, he had still been the businessman who had come to pass the time at a music hall and who, even there, found it hard to forget and disengage himself from the current of his familiar ideas, only amusing himself in the measure that, as it did this evening, the exterior gaiety served to increase an intimate contentment, in accord with the joy of a success and reinforcing it.

From the moment when La P ascalieri came on stage, however, he knew, perhaps for the first time in his existence, the total absorption of his being by the external, the complete participation in an action half-material and half-imaginary, the clear, total and absolute perception of an esthetic emotion that certain more favored people experience in other places and for other objects. It was not that he had not declared, as is only fitting, when the occasion presented itself, that a landscape was beautiful, or admired a painting or a poem, or applauded a few celebrated melodies during a concert; nevertheless, in reality, no effective color had ever tinted judgments of that sort as powerfully for him.

When the curtain, after multiple recalls, fell definitively on La Pascalieri's triumphant smile, Jim Broks still retained the disturbance of that profound, poignant interior emotion, new for him, which surprised him, and which he strove to dissimulate as he dragged his companion to the bar.

In the corridors the entr'acte was pouring out its flood of strollers. Reality was affirmed again, furnishing its customary contingent of benchmarks, to the measure of which the proportions of the previous scenes were reduced. They resumed their place in the series of habitual events. The oppressions they had caused dissipated. That flight into the infinity of dream and toward beauty shrank to the dimensions of a "topic of conversation."

Wirsea, who had just lit a cigar, commenced between two puffs.

"Wasn't I right to tell you that she was marvelous? In Vienna she only danced in a small number of songs and dances, accompanied by a troupe of musicians on the stage: violins, guitars and mandolins."

Jim Broks ordered champagne.

"Already," Wirsea continued, "she was a success. But here, what a triumph, that pantomime! And you know, the music was composed by a master, the libretto by an Academician. She's worth that, truly."

Jim Broks approved, adding: "I understand now why all artists talk about Paris, and want so much to be produced in Paris: I thought that realizing such a great and beautiful thing on a music hall stage would be impossible. More than that, I'm ashamed to admit it, but I ought to declare that I seem better able now to comprehend that famous word 'art,' and what it signifies, than after an evening at Covent Garden."

Their conversation deviated to the last opera season, and they were laughing together at a performance producing, alongside an obese Romeo, a chanteuse interpreting the role of Juliet who was not only fat but the age of a grandmother, when the bell rang announcing the end of the entr'acte,

Wirsea and Jim Broks emptied one last glass and then, in a very good humor, returned to their box. Already the footlights were illuminating the enormous branches of a cherry tree, with strings of pink silk flowers over a décor of black satin embroidered with naïve perspectives: curved bridges circled torrents with whiteness, while in the background, the traditional Fuji raised its snowy cone above a well of blue canvas and a tumble of small houses emerging from foliage.

The program announced: *No. 9 —The Hakamura Family; Japanese acrobats.*

Five small individuals in magical robes advanced, sumptuous and very grave, and then prostrated themselves in a ceremonial salute.

At the sight of them, Jim Broks' gaiety suddenly gave way to an abrupt malaise. A kind of inexplicable commotion shook him. He thought: *They resemble terribly the man who was writing in my dream. A man like those replied to the other: "The Japanese, in that epoch, only knew wood and charcoal."*

Yes, he was Japanese, and the country where people were astonished by stones that burned—black stones—was his country! I'm certain that he was writing in that room. Why, then, did I talk about my *room to Faxton, when telling him the story?*

But in that case, I wasn't dreaming! How would I have been able, in that case, to recognize here that the man who was writing was like these, the man that Faxton asked me to describe, the man that I never saw?

However, it seemed to me that it was me! Oh, my God me, Japanese! For I wasn't dreaming...I have the certainty of having lived that... elsewhere! Where? In what world? My God, my God, am I going mad?

Under the shock of that revelation, Jim suddenly went pale, vacillating in his armchair.

Wirsea, who had been looking at him for an instant, was worried by his pallor and his fixed gaze, and took his hands. "What's the matter, my dear?" he asked. "Don't you feel very well?"

"Pay no attention," Jim Broks replied, in a faint voice. "In fact, I don't really know what I'm feeling. Doubtless it's the fatigue of the voyage. I'm desolate but...it would be better, I think, if I returned to my hotel. You'll excuse me."

"Of course," said Wirsea. "Anyway, I'll accompany you."

"Not at all, not at all! I won't permit you to disturb yourself. I don't believe that I'm suffering; I only need a little rest. I'm so sorry to quit you that I wouldn't want to deprive you of the spectacle as well. Stay, I beg you, and forgive me. A good night will set me right."

"At any rate, I'll come to see you tomorrow morning."

"Be assured that I'll be entirely well. Anyway, I'll telephone you early in order to save you any disturbance."

Before going to bed, Jim reflected at length. He saw Mansur Cottage again, his sister, Cyrus Humber, that chilly day in May,[9] Norman, Bob and Nelly, playing boisterously around their uncle, and then the spade abandoned next to the box-tree hedge, his gesture to put it on his head, which had provoked so much hilarity in the children... and then the double life, by which various impressions were superimposed on the real environment that were perceived by an individual sitting in a chair and writing at a table.... Above all, the baroque conviction persisted that he was simultaneously the man who was writing and Jim Broks, kneeling on the sand of a pathway in his brother-in-law's garden, playing with his nephews and his niece.

Now he had collided with another mysterious event.

Why had the entrance on stage of Japanese acrobats caused him such a shock?

Invoking the first disturbance that had seized him before the marvelous information of La Pascalieri, teaching him the profound significance of art and beauty, was insufficient explanation, as was the slight intoxication of a few glasses of champagne.

That commotion, which had contracted his heart so forcefully and withdrawn all the blood from his face, evidently originated from the fact that the five Japanese had unexpectedly brought him the immediate certainty, the absolute conviction, that the man who was writing

---

[9] The author appears to have forgotten recording at the beginning of the story that the temperature on the day in question was "almost summery."

was similar to them. At present, that certainty, initially acquired by a kind of intuition, was fortified in such a manner that he could not dispute it or doubt it, because new details were gradually returning to his memory now. He remembered the form and the color of the small brown hand that was agitating on the paper. Certainly, those fingers did not belong to a European; the European in the room had been standing up.

Furthermore, a sign had marked the top of the page. He could have drawn it:

$$+$$
$$-$$
$$-$$

All that, a dream?

No! Judge was mistaken. In a dream, a real grand piano encumbered by trinkets, in its real place, real children's cries, a real lawn, that ensemble of chords struck forcefully and without a false note on the keyboard of the senses, could not coexist with another décor, above all an imaginary décor.

And Jim, pausing before the cupboard in his room, perceived at that moment in the mirror a phantom with his resemblance, with shining, haggard eyes, a livid, bewildered face and disorderly clothes.

"I look like a madman!" he murmured, sobbing. "They talk like this in a loud voice. They gesticulate. They have hallucinations.

"Awaiting madness, that's my future!

"Awaiting it... and hiding its progress! They dissimulate, Judge said... for a long time, perhaps for years.

"My God! My God!"

He threw himself on the bed, fully dressed, without daring to switch off the lights, and went to sleep, his face moist with tears, thinking that it would be necessary tomorrow to possess the requisite courage to play the drama, not to let a single word escape that might raise the alert.

Above all, Judge, whom he had already informed so maladroitly, must not suspect anything.

V. The Boom

Five weeks after Jim Broks' journey to Paris, the financial situation of the two associates had been modified considerably.

The successive cablegrams announcing the completion of the railway from the mine to the sea, its inauguration, honored by the presence of a Peruvian minister, and the dispatch of the first cargoes of nitrate, had rapidly determined an exaggerated shift in demand for Peruvian Nitrate shares, in one of those movements frequent on the Stock Exchange, which provoked a rise as excessive as the previous drop had been unjustified. There was no one among those who had been in such haste to get rid of the stock who did not want to obtain some. The speculation was hectic, to such a degree that the share price began to reach utterly unreasonable levels. In spite of the approach of the vacation, it continued to rise a few points every day.

Only one man took account of the risks implicit in the situation, and that was Faxton Judge; but he lavished advice to be prudent on his clients in vain; the enthusiasm was so forceful that some wrote him bitter letters accusing him of having a personal interest in a drop.

Until the month of July, the firm of Broks and Judge had not sold a single one of its numerous Peruvian Nitrate shares, which, in contributing to maintain the scarcity of the share in the market, had aided that exaggerated rise.

Old Sam Lane, rendered proud by success, was triumphant with regard to his friends, whom he had advised to buy in mid-fall. Sure of the real value of his affair, he never ceased to repeat to Jim, who had told him that morning what his associate had said: "Above all, don't let any go! Don't sell a single share; you'll repent of it later."

"He's exaggerating," Judge replied, distractedly.

In other circumstances, he would have explained to Jim at length that even if Peruvian Nitrate were quoted one day at twice its present figure and that price were absolutely justified—which Judge did not believe—it would be no less true that the present infatuation would inevitably be succeeded by a reaction, the amplitude and duration of which it was difficult to predict.

Nevertheless, out of respect for the special situation of Jim with regard to old Sam, he would probably have decided only to sell the block of shares bought from Wirsea and to keep the large quantity that they held in addition. It would have been in conformity with his habits of prudence to secure by that conduct both the self-esteem of Sam Lane and the interests of Broks and Judge, which could not reasonably leave the major part of its funds immobilized indefinitely in Peruvian Nitrate.

Since the rise, however, Faxton Judge had been subject to a terrible temptation. A hundred times already he had calculated the sum that their participation represented, swollen by events; a hundred times he had been on the point of explaining to his associate that it was imprudent to remain so considerably engaged. However, he had kept silent.

That was because the sage, intelligent and clairvoyant Faxton could not succeed in recovering the sang-froid, calm, lucidity and promptitude of decision that habitually conferred in him an overwhelming superiority over his colleagues, even the most skillful. Perhaps for the first time in his life, he could measure the degree of power that certain sentiments are susceptible of acquiring and what restrictions they impose on the free exercise of thought.

His ordinary occupations were accomplished mechanically, without appetite or pleasure; another individual had been born on the evening of Double-Head's confession, and had grown, agitated, reasoned and suffered within him, different from the broker Faxton Judge.

That individual, proud of knowing himself to be the holder of a unique secret, a marvelous talisman, was harassed by a perpetual desire to test its power. He looked at the world with new eyes, sensed swelling in his heart a vague enormous scorn for people he passed in the street, whose peers he had ceased to be. For he alone possessed the key permitting the deciphering of a hieroglyph of the universal mystery, an arcanum over which so many scholars had stumbled, or which they thought they had translated clearly when, in reality, they had committed to most ludicrous error in labeling "telepathic" hallucinations that were no different from ordinary hallucinations.

"Tell me, my dear Jim," he asked, after a silence, "how Peruvian is doing today."

"It opened at 7 13/16. Yesterday's closing quite was 7 ¾. It'll certainly finish at 8. All the same, Faxton, if Wirsea had been able to foresee these prices, and the Lawsons! Do you remember!?"

"Do you think it very wise," Judge interrupted abruptly, "to continue not to realize anything? Are you truly of the opinion that we should follow Sam Lane's indications to the letter? In sum, the excellent man has the means to wait; he has no immediate interest in selling; but is it the same for us? I don't think so,"

"However," said Jim, "I talked to you about our position last week, and you said 'There's no urgency.' Oughtn't we to wait another week. In a week, it'll probably go up another ten shillings. That's almost this week's plus-value."

"The rise can't be prolonged indefinitely, remember."

"Assuredly. Nevertheless, we're not yet at the point where the price is remaining stationary."

"With a slightly prolonged flow of sales it wouldn't remain stationary for long."

"The market is relatively healthy. Where would that flow of sales come from, my dear Faxton, and how would it be prolonged? In sum, Wirsea's package doesn't appear to me to be any more difficult to let out next week than today, and as we can scarcely..."

"Hmm! We can scarcely...?"

Judge hesitated for a moment after that remark. That was sufficient for his associate, struck by the embarrassed fashion in which he had lowered his head, exclaimed:

"What, Faxton! You also want to sell Lowdes and William Rose—in brief, everything we were forced to buy when the Lawsons were threatening to demolish everything?"

Judge remained silent.

"What!" Jim went on, in an astonished murmur. "Even more? Everything!"

"Everything," repeated Judge, softly. "Yes, everything."

He waited, slightly anxiously, for he expected a rather sharp reaction on the part of his associate, of protests inspired by the dread of displeasing Sam Lane—a sentiment that Jim had conserved very keenly.

That was because Judge did not suspect the terrible fashion in which Double-Head had been affected by an evening commenced in the company of Wirsea in the music hall during his short trip to Paris. For weeks, unknown to Faxton, Jim had continued to watch anxiously for the return of a crisis. Observing nothing abnormal, he had been gradually reassured, but he conserved lugubrious apprehensions deep inside himself.

That latent fear dominated him too much, and he was, on the other hand too habituated to considering Judge and a kind of leader whose indications ought to be followed scrupulously, for him to have the kind of revolt that Faxton had feared before the brutal expression of an opinion so diametrically opposed to that of Sam Lane, the revered benefactor, and the grand master of Peruvian Nitrate.

After a long silence, Jim Broks contented himself with saying: "In sum, before deciding anything, it would be good to see exactly what our position is in the share."

As he was about to ring to ask for the books, Judge stopped him with a gesture, and, opening a drawer in his desk, he took out a small notebook.

"I have all the figures here," he said. "Have you imagined the sum represented by our participation at current prices?"

Jim responded swiftly: "It's pointless to calculate thus. In any case, we can't dispose of shares inscribed in our name on the company registers."

"Of course."

Judge was beginning to be prodigiously surprised. He was still prepared to encounter in Jim a serious resistance, an opposition that it would be necessary to combat, and now his associate, without the slightest objection—for Faxton had never thought of selling the fifty shares to which Jim was alluding—was capitulating without even a fight. In that, again, Judge recognized "a sign" that rejoiced his new soul, that of a gambler. Decidedly, destiny was manifesting its determination to encourage him; "luck" was continuing to accompany him.

In reality, there was in Jim, in addition to his habitual confidence in Faxton, the terror of the frightful malady, engendering the desire, unconfessed but powerful, to profit from this unexpected opportunity, this fortune that might offer a means of escaping madness.

Furthermore, although his most optimistic anticipations had never envisaged the reimbursement of the partnership advanced by Sam Lane, as well as the constitution of a personal wealth sufficient to procure him a complete independence, except after many years, the marvelous rise brought him the possibility of abridging, in a matter of days, as if by waving a magic wand, the duration of that long period of toil and waiting, rendered even more painful by the recent accident and the perpetual menace of a repetition.

However, Jim had never dared to talk first to Faxton about the realization of their Peruvian Nitrate shares, for that operation appeared to him, in spite of everything, to be immoral. Would it not be necessary, in fact, in order to accomplish it, to go against the wishes of his benefactor, Sam Lane, and to fear being accused by clients of ridding themselves of a share that they had been advised to buy.

Nevertheless, as soon as Judge spoke, poor Double-Head had felt any appetite for struggle abandoning him; his hesitations had fled. After all, was madness not lying in wait for him? Could he struggle against business and madness at the same time? Did he not, on the contrary, have a duty and a right to try to care for himself, to cure himself? A timid hope germinated within him.

The two associates, who had, each for his own part, been greatly afraid of one another, thus found themselves in perfect accord, although it was for completely different and carefully hidden intimate reasons.

A few days later, the important operation was terminated, without having provoked anything more than a halt in the rise, followed by the commencement of a reaction, which was judged very natural and quickly suppressed.

Jim's scruples then commenced to seem simply ridiculous. He found nothing scandalous in that rapid enrichment, which, on the contrary, procured him a sense of honest equilibrium, security and wellbeing.

As for Judge, he refrained once again from raising the question about which he thought incessantly. He observed with satisfaction the ingenuous joy of his associate and limited himself to awaiting the moment he judged favorable, fearing to compromise everything by too much haste. Meanwhile, he persuaded Jim, without too much difficulty, to leave the care of current affairs, which the approach of the vacation rendered rare anyway, to a proxy. That way, they could take a little trip to the continent together.

Jim, who was far less interested in the Stock Exchange now that he considered the ordinary produce of their firm as a sort of supplementary revenue, accepted that plan.

In a fortnight, everything was arranged.

Judge took advantage of that time to have the apparatus constructed, in separate sections confided to different firms, that he had sketched so often and then re-

touched be fore c ompleting t hem. F inally, he w as e nter-
ing the period of realization!

Large gratifications accelerated the completion of
the w ork, f urther facilitated by i ts d ivision, so suc cess-
fully t hat, two da ys be fore t he da te fixed f or t he de par-
ture, four crates were added to the radiant Faxton's baggage.

On t he o ther ha nd, C yrus H umber's pa rticipation
had r ealized a g ood p rofit, unde r the pr etext that they
could not c onfide the surveillance o f that capital to a
proxy.

With regard to Sam Lane, Jim had attributed his recent fortune to the s uccess of a bi g ope ration in A merican Railways, while proposing the reimbursement of
three-quarters of his partnership.

The na ïve f ellow ha d dreaded t hat i nterview, f earing indiscreet questions and a possible refusal, but, contrary to his pe ssimistic ant icipations, Sam L ane ha d accepted immediately, signed the receipt pr epared by
Judge and banked the funds, contenting himself with the
summary explanations furnished by his debtor.

In e xchange f or hi s m oney a nd hi s w arm t hanks,
Jim r eceived from hi s be nefactor t he as surance t hat the
latter ha d never doub ted his suc cess, especially w ith an
associate o f t he v alue of F axton Judge—in spite of
which he w as ab le to observe that the old and rich Sam
Lane s eemed happily su rprised r ather than di scontented
to recover a pa rt o f hi s ca pital i nstead of i nterest pa y-
ments, a lbeit de livered p unctually. S o J im t ook a d-
vantage of those good dispositions to let it be understood
that in a few m onths, w ithout a doubt, i f nothing unfortunate oc curred, he would be abl e t o liberate himself
from the rest of his debt.

Sam L ane r esponded to h im, c heerfully t his t ime, while s haking hi s ha nd: "There's n o hu rry f or t hat set-tlement, my dear friend; whenever you wish will be fine. Choose y our m oment, f or I w ouldn't w ant y ou t o put yourself out for me."

VI. Vacation

On the deck of the ship that was getting ready to set sail for Ostend, Jim, his double head coiffed in an elegant check cap, gazed at the calm and smiling Judge enviously, for the voyage, the first he had undertaken that was not for business, was not giving him all the pleasure he had promised himself. The program of visiting Belgium and Holland already seemed less attractive to his activity than the ordinary and quotidian lot of imminent and remunerative goals, rapidly accomplished tasks, transactions translated in precise figures, commissions and profits.

And yet, how many times had he cursed telephone calls, the change, clients, and the slavery in which the debt contracted to old Sam Lane held him: the prospect of years of monotonous labor, disturbance and fatigue, only punctuated by weekly visits to his sister, the relaxation of Sunday and a few evenings at the theater?

Thus, during the last few weeks, he had savored fully the pleasure of his recent fortune. An incomparable ease lightened every day the weight of former cares. The hours only chimed for him in cheerful carillons. Now, the new joy of triumph was being slowly extinguished. In its place, a vague melancholy had insinuated itself into Jim's heart, increasing with every turn of the propeller, growing as the steamer drew away from the white cliffs of Dover.

He drew nearer to his associate.

"Really," he said, "I admire you. You seem to be the very image of happiness, while I'm striving in vain to attain it. I know that I ought to be content to be departing on vacation for an interesting voyage, and I was just a little while ago…"

"And what has changed now?"

"I can't define it; I only feel a sort of lassitude, almost a slight sadness, when I ought not to be experiencing such sentiments, and I'm embarrassed by them."

"Let's see, Jim, are you regretting…?"

"Not having conserved a few Peruvian Nitrates? Certainly not. I think it's rather that I don't have the habit of taking holidays. I can't take such a long rest without a certain remorse. Spending money without earning any doesn't cheer me up either. This kind of displacement, without a business meeting on arrival, causes me a vague unease; to dissipate it, to calm my scruples. I need to repeat that what I'm doing is excellent for my health. Isn't it?"

"Assuredly."

"Then the impression changes slightly, while remaining fundamentally disagreeable, for I don't have a good memory of any remedy. As a child, I gave a great deal of trouble to my poor mother when I was ill and it was necessary to make me swallow medicine."

Judge could not repress a frank burst of laughter. "Hmm! How dare you, my poor friend, compare this sky, this sunlight and this rocking on the swell, these minutes of exquisite idleness in the marine wind, to some nauseating drug?"

"Go on, then! It's necessary to be mad…!"

"No, Jim. I wouldn't want to say anything like that, even in jest."

"But as for me, I assure you, Faxton, I think about it seriously. Unfortunately, I possess solid enough reasons to justify that idea. Besides which, if you remember, it isn't the first time that I've expressed anxieties of t hat sort to you."

He took an armchair, sat down next Judge and continued: " After a ll, now th at m y s ituation in regard to Sam L ane i s r egulated, a nd our ow n pos ition h as changed so advantageously and become solid, c lear and prosperous, I have less dread…and would even be glad to c ontinue the c onfidences that y ou c ommenced t o accumulate on a certain weekend in May."

"The S aturday w hen y ou t old m e t he s tory of a…singular dream?"

"Extravagant would be a more exact term, for I 've acquired subsequently t he certainty t hat t he d isturbance that bowled me over couldn't be explained by a dream, as you supposed."

"How?" Judge i nterrogated, a ll t he m ore s urprised because he too remembered Rimney's visit. In spite of his promise to return s oon, the scatterbrained Rimney had not reappeared at the Saint B arnaby Building; he had not, therefore, communicated with Jim.

The latter continued his confession. He retraced the evening spent at the music hall in Paris with Wirsea, described the magical appearance of L a Pascalieri, the unaccustomed e motion t hat he ha d felt be fore t he pe rformance of t he celebrated artiste, and, above all, the revelation of her beauty—or, rather, of Beauty. Then he described the shock he had experienced, the sort of influx of s trange r eminiscences, caused by t he v ision o f t he Japanese acrobats as soon as they came on stage.

"Suddenly," he said, "it seemed to me that an intolerable light illuminated certain corners of my brain that had remained obscure until then, in the sense that it immediately became easy for me to respond to the questions y ou had a sked m e f ruitlessly, a nd w hich h ad n ot previously taken on any significance for me. I sensed, at that precise moment…I knew…it was revealed to me, that I had *lived*—do you understand, Faxton?—*lived* and not *dreamed* the brief series of actions that I had reconstituted for you with such difficulty.

"So, you can easily imagine my amazement and my anguish when that terrible truth stunned me with its unexpected weight..."

Judge tried to speak, but Jim imposed silence on him with a gesture.

"Oh, you won't convince me now as you did the first time. I'm not unaware that stories of that kind abound in the matter of dementia; I've read a few books of mental medicine since then. There are those who believe themselves to be messengers of God, heroes, emperors, kings. There are also those who imagine that the substance of their body has been transformed into glass, chocolate or metal... Well, my delirium of a few minutes would doubtless have led me, had it been prolonged, to incarnating within me some samurai…the one whose small brown hand I saw…but won't the samurai come back one day?"

"Hmm," said Judge. "I don't think so,"

"Why not?" said his associate, sharply. "Evidently, I've passed several months without a relapse, but not without dread. Now, this melancholy that's increasing the further we draw away from London and Dover, when no apparent cause legitimates it, I fear having to attribute an unfortunate significance to it. Perhaps it's announcing to me the imminent return of a new crisis. Anyway, Faxton, you're now up to date, and if anything happens..."

"Don't worry, Jim. Nothing more will happen that will frighten you. I repeat to you that your case doesn't

offer a ny a larming s ymptom, a nd t hat it d oesn't approach, in any respect, the examples that you cite."

"What!"

"You heard correctly: t he s amurai w ill only l ive
again in y ou and by m eans of you if y ou consent to it.
Otherwise, ne ver! Anyway, you'll s oon understand m e.
In the same w ay that you've hi dden your Parisian crisis
from me, I've left you in ignorance of a very significant
detail."

In hi s t urn, Judge s poke, r eveling t he f ashion i n
which R imney's v isit had s timulated his hypothesis of a
telepathic c ommunication, a hypothesis immediately
verified, since, at t he time when Jim had experienced
that s trange doubl ing of personality i n the g arden of
Mansur C ottage, not f ar away, sitting at a t able in the
middle of the room pe rceived confusedly by J im,
Rimney's J apanese pupil really had been writing the exact phrases relative to stones that burn.

By means of a skillful t ransition, Judge then
broached the proposition that interested him.

"I'm not a sking y ou, my de ar friend, to believe me
blindly w hen I a ffirm t o y ou t hat, i n m y opi nion, you
posses a r are pow er, w hose di scovery ha s bow led y ou
over, which is quite natural, and if I affirm that your pre-
tended malady i s r educible t o an une xpected en trance
into communication with a foreign soul..."

"By means of a m agic w ooden spoon," Jim specified, smiling.

"Hmm! It would, in fact, be easy for you to try that
means ag ain...or, better, a s lightly i mproved m ethod.
What would it cost you to lend yourself to a few experiments?"

"Of the s ort that y ou already de sired to attempt in
your kitchen? Do you remember?"

"Yes. But you'd gain this time by being rid of your fears, acquiring the conviction that I'm not enticing you, and that I'm not mistaken myself. Finally, we also have a chance of acquiring, without any special wire and outside all agencies, sensational news of which we'd be well placed—recognize it—to profit."

Jim Broks remained silent for a few moments.

The English shore no longer appeared as anything but a vague mist tarnishing the sky on the horizon. Between that thin strip of fog and the steamer, the mobile water extended, striped with foam, over which a few trawlers moved heavily.

Jim gazed alternately at the thousand gold spangles that the sunlight scattered over the crests of the waves, the heavy hulls swaying gently under their ocher sails and smoke, the seagulls escorting the ship, and his associate, who was waiting for his response impatiently. He smiled, inhaled the air, salted by the spray, deeply, and finally said:

"You're a marvelous physician, I think, my dear Faxton. I believe that I am, if not entirely better, at least well on the way to a cure. I'm already much better, I assure you. My irritating melancholy is fading away, like the shoes of our dear homeland at present. So I'd truly be an ingrate if I refused you what you expect of me. You can experiment as much as you please. On that subject, tell me, what if we were to renounce our voyage to Holland in order to rent a comfortable little villa on the Belgian coast? Perhaps it would be more amusing to experiment thus to travel as tourists, and we'd waste less time."

That proposal responded too well to Judge's secret desires for him not to give it an immediate and enthusiastic adhesion. It was therefore decided that they would abandon the visit to the Dutch museums, the excursions to Volendam, the Zuyder Zee and the isle of Marken for the joys of experimentation, siestas on the sand dunes, and bathing.

As soon as they arrived, hazard served them as they wished; they found quite rapidly, a short distance from the town, facing the sea, a neat, bright and cheerful detached house. It was inhabited by the widow of an art dealer, who, in order to augment her income, which had been diminished by the death of her husband, rented out two spacious and comfortably furnished rooms situated on the first floor.

The husband's former studios subsisted at the end of the garden, behind the house, and possessed a private exit to a side-street. They had comprised two juxtaposed hangars of unequal height, which had been subsequently been enclosed completely, equipped with glazed windows and partition walls. A part of the lower section was used as a laundry and fuel-store; the rest, forming a room that had served as a storeroom, was provided with a floor, and communicated with the more elevated of the two buildings by a door, still striped with multiple brush-strokes, displaying a furious spectrum of bright colors. A few empty shelves, a table of black wood and three wicker chairs comprised the entire furniture. The other room, with a floor of beaten earth, carefully sanded, remained completely bare.

When he discovered those outbuildings at the corner of a path, and had visited then, the enthused Judge quickly fell into accord with the proprietor, who was pleased by the serious appearance of the two men and included those facilities in the price that was agreed.

He was soon assured of the excellence of his choice, and certain that he would be able to operate without fear of ind iscretions; the widow Lansaert and her o ld Flemish maidservant testified no curiosity r egarding the contents of the crates that accompanied the visitors' ordinary baggage.

Their reserve w as not be lied du ring the few days the Judge e mployed i n s etting up hi s a pparatus. I n t he morning, M adame L ansaert was oc cupied in her house-work; the a fternoon w as c onsecrated t o a w alk on t he dike and then watering the flowers i n her garden, for which she cared with a particular solicitude. She seemed to avoid encountering her guests, by virtue of a exagger-ated sentiment of politeness, a nd t hey divined t hat s he would h ave bl ushed at the t hought of a ddressing t he slightest question to them. As for Rosa, the confection of tasty meals, the cleaning of t he furniture, the floors and the c oppers, a pe rpetual c oncern w ith m eticulous ne at-ness, and, in m oments of l eisure, r eading *The K ey t o Dreams*, sufficed to absorb her physical and intellectual activity completely.

Cheered up by the unexpected turn that his vacation was taking, Jim Broks, as the unpacking proceeded, ad-mired F axton's i ngenuity. He he lped h im, very a mused by the collections of wooden lenses, to classify them by species, and arrange them in good order on t he s helves of the former storeroom. Then it was the turn of the var-ious pi eces o f the app aratus, which i t w as ne cessary t o assemble.

Meals, bathing and evenings at t he Kursaal inter-rupted the assemblage s essions, i n the c ourse of w hich, absorbed by a labor that was rather finicky, the two as-sociates sc arcely exc hanged more w ords t han were i n-dispensable.

When everything was ready, the connections of the mechanism adjusted and the lens-bearing tripods erected like bizarre spiders, Judge revised the articulations and gears a few more times, verified the alignments, maneuvered the rowels and the switches, tightened a few screws, and then approached the table on which he had disposed geographical maps on several scales, compasses, protractors, a magnetic compass and a stack of white paper. Suddenly, he replaced in his pocket the chronometer that he had just taken out and addressed Jim.

"Hmm!" he said. "This is the moment so long desired, and...I dare not give the signal to depart...to depart for the unknown! I'm simultaneously anxious and cheerful, certainly very emotional...too much for this work. My dear Jim, I regret perhaps giving you the impression of a capricious eccentric, when in reality I only desire to reconquer the calm, tranquil coolness befitting an observer of suc h..." He hesitated over the word to pronounce. "...Possibility, isn't it?" he ended up saying. "For we're about to attempt the impossible. Tomorrow, do you think? Tomorrow morning, we'll begin."

"You know," replied Double-Head, "that I'm entirely at your disposal, my dear friend. Nevertheless, permit me to ask you whether your stopping like this, at the last moment, isn't a sort of stifled protestation of your conscience? After all, do you think that what we're about to attempt to do is very moral? Pardon me for a frankness assuredly too brutal in its manner of expression, but I don't want to mask or diminish the sentiment that I've just experienced. It seems to me—or, rather your hesitation has led me to think—that we're acting here a little like two honest men who, as a game, have laid out in front of them a whole set of burglar's tools and who, gripped by scruples, are recoiling before utilizing them."

"What a singular comparison! A nd what s cruples are you talking about?" replied Judge, who, entirely oc-cupied with the realization of his plans, attentive to the quotidian labor, had never, in fact, envisaged that aspect of the question. His eyes, candid and surprised, scanned the varnished copper, the rigid feet, the scattered tools, as if to take them as witnesses to the exclusively scien-tific quality of his intentions. He seemed visibly shocked by Jim's suggestion.

The later continued: " I'm s orry t o ha ve t roubled you s o m uch. H owever, F axton, reflect. W hat a re we proposing to accomplish?"

"An attempt at telepathy, at the true communication of thought without an intermediary, something sincere, clear and exact, different from all the poor boasts that have decorated our ambitions in vain without succeeding in legitimating their birth. Are you and I not bringing, by contrast, a complete probity in our enterprise?"

"Assuredly—but the enterprise itself tends, in sum, to penetrate into the brain, the soul, of another, without the authorization of its proprietor, Faxton! We're seek-ing to capture the most hidden thoughts of a person, un-known to him. Do you understand now? It's evidently not a matter of stealing pearl necklaces or cash, of break-ing into a safe. However, can't appropriating ideas and secrets like that, sometimes more precious than jewels or bonds, which are similarly believed to be secure, shel-tered from all seizure, also be validly considered as a theft?"

"Hmm...! Hmm...! Let's not exaggerate. I concede to you, my dear friend, that there might *theoretically* be material there for superb dissertations for a preacher or a professor of philosophy. Practically, numerous gentle-men, from Heads of State, ministers, ambassadors and generals t o t he l east o f reporters, without f orgetting some of our colleagues on the Stock Exchange, enjoy a perfect consideration and are held to be very honorable. Now, Jim, agree that they employ means in order to inform t hemselves f ar m ore i mmoral t han these hone st instruments!"

"Certainly!"

"In consequence, given that, if we succeed in obtaining results, we will never utilize them with a view to guilty e nds, b lackmail, e tc., t he e xperiment t hat w e're proposing to carry out remains perfectly legitimate. And with this, I think it's high time to go and have tea."

Rosa c ame t o s erve i t in the d ining r oom, w hich was cool and semi-dark.

Through the closed shutters, a slight odor of carnations, honeysuckle and r oses f lirted, e scaping f rom t he sunlit garden and coming to be confounded with the perfume of t he bou quets whose s plendor painted the bronzed pottery of the F lemish dresser with colored reflections.

Usually, Madame Lansaert was waiting for the two men in order to take tea with them; that day her place was empty. Thus, when the young widow came in, a few minutes later, offering the e xcuse of having pr olonged her ha bitual w alk, J im c onsidered h er, a nd br ought a n unaccustomed attention to that examination. Very supple in he r bl ack dr ess, s he t ook of f he r ha t w ith r apid but harmonious gestures. Rebellious blonde cu rls escaped, which she had not constrained to the ordinary obedience.

The heat outside and emotion painted her face with a redness that transfigured her, adding a brighter light to her brown eyes and a touch of crimson to her lips. And when the two associates took their leave of their hostess, Double-Head, a fter be ing m ute f or a r ather long t ime,

91

said to Judge, who, absorbed by his own thoughts relative to the famous experiment, had respected his silence: "I hadn't perceived before that our hostess is a pretty woman... a very pretty woman, in fact!"

VII. Extracts from Judge's Journal

...Certain kinds of phot ographic a pparatus give a clear image, without being focused, on the sole condition of interposing between them and the object to be reproduced a distance that can vary from infinity to three meters, or even one meter fifty, and equipping them, in the later c ase, with a su pplementary l ens. I ha ve m easured the length of the line that separated, as the crow flies, the room of Mitsugawa, Rimney's Japanese student, from the garden of Cyrus Humber, and I found it to be about 53 7 yards. N evertheless, I t hought t hat a s horter di s-tance, for t he r eason of g reater exp osure, offers no inconvenience and would be preferable with regard to the first trial.

I therefore decided to begin with a reading, which I would make in the room that had served as a storeroom, the communicating for g iving access t o the main studio being c losed. I n t he pa rt of t he n otebook r eserved f or measurements a nd technical observations. I ha ve not ed precisely how I took my reference points, orientated the apparatus and how I disposed Jim and placed myself. In order to avoid any error and facilitate checking, I did not tell Jim what I intended to do, only asking him, if a phenomenon similar to the one at Mansur Cottage was produced, to record as faithfully as possible what he sensed. In consequence, I provided him with what he needed to relate his impressions.

For m y pa rt, I e quipped m yself, w ithout h is knowledge, with a v olume of pr ose. I bor rowed it from Madame L ansaert, asking he r to choose a book at r an-dom from a little bookcase that I had noticed ornamenting a corner of her drawing room. She handed me the second volume of a French translation of a work by Dickens entitled *The Old Curiosity Shop.*

Jim was to put on the special helmet at twenty past eleven.

At the precise moment, I inserted my index finger between two pages, which opened. I therefore began to read the left hand page, number 166, which was completely unknown to me, attentively: "...pence in a saucer, and adjusting the poor candle, the cards once shuffled and cut, here are the stakes. If you win, you get everything; if I win; it's mine. To make the game more amusing and more comical, I shall call you the Marquise, do you understand?"[10]

I thought it as well, remembering what Jim had told me about the disturbance that his first communication had caused him, not to go any further. In addition, it's necessary to confess, I was impatient to know whether that first attempt, scrupulously prepared, had succeeded.

In the studio I found Jim immobile, his eyelids lowered, his featured contracted. He did not budge when I advanced. My soles however, creaking on the sand, ought to have warned him of my presence. I observed him momentarily; he conserved that attitude of absolute insensibility, which conferred such rigidity on his entire being that I wondered whether he might be plunged in hypnotic sleep and fallen into catalepsy. At any rate, it became evident that my trial had failed pitifully insofar as the transmission of phrases of Dickens were concerned.

---

[10] The back-translated quotation is from chapter LV of the French translation, which does not correspond to chapter 55 of the original; the speaker is Dick Swiveller.

In spite of that, I experienced less chagrin than a sort of ironic commiseration with regard to my defunct hopes. How, in fact, had I had the candor to hope to succeed so easily? And what stupid conceit had led me to suppose that the direction I had imprinted on my research for that first experiment would be advantageous? I had evidently exaggerated the value of my inductions, estimated at too low a tariff the part of chance and, in sum, taken a false route. Instead of commanding events as a master without further ado, I had to resign myself temporarily to remaining their humble slave. But I was already thinking about exploiting the error and drawing a profit from the information that the unexpected turn taken by events would bring me. For that, I needed to observe the slightest circumstances attentively.

What, then, was happening?

I did not take long to find out. A few minutes later, Double-Head took off the apparatus.

Holding in one of his hands the pencil I had given him, while agitating pieces of paper in the other, virgin of all writing, he started gesticulating in an incoherent manner, capering joyfully, and laughing in bursts, to end up striking me on the shoulder, declaring to me: "Marvelous, my old comrade, your invention! Clear vision, clear audition; sensations perfectly perceived! Very amusing, you know, your machine for traveling in brains and capturing thoughts."

"I can see," I said, very emotional, "that you've obtained a telepathic communication."

"Immediately."

"Frankly, Jim, my pleasure as an inventor is doubled by that caused to me by the certainty of knowing that you're definitively liberated from your fears. I assume that you no longer have any fear of the samurai now?"

"You're right, my dear Faxton, and I thank you. The proof is made now, for the hallucination was produced in exactly the same fashion as in the garden of Mansur Cottage; but this time I wasn't afraid, and for greater convenience, I closed my ordinary eyes."

"And what did your second eyes see?"

"It's rather complicated to describe. I'd prefer to translate and summarize it for you right away. It is, in fact, pointless for me to enumerate my slightest impressions in detail, as I did the first time. However, I declare to you that it was thanks to chance that I know *who I was living*, if I might put it thus—the hazard of a little pocket mirror consulted; it confirmed the supposition that I had made on hearing the sound of the voice. You don't understand very well? Yes, that's the inconvenience of your apparatus; one doesn't know, at first who one is, nor where one is. Inconvenient, isn't it? Fortunately, in this instance, I know that. It's a matter of La Pascalieri, the artiste about whom I spoke to you in such an enthusiast manner on my return from Paris, if you remember."

"But according to you, she doesn't play comic roles, so I can't explain your exuberant gaiety."

"At the theater, certainly, she plays drama. In the city, I can now affirm, she excels in comedy, as witness the scene in which I've just taken part in the office of the director of the Spa Casino—the posters plastered on the wall informed me immediately of the name of the town.

"At the moment when I put on the helmet, that gentleman received a piece of paper from the hands of La Pascalieri, which she was holding out to him. He read in a loud voice this, which I've retained very well: 'Very

sorry to know you absent from Paris, a departing immediately, desirous of coming to applaud you this evening
and thereafter. Harriman.' He added: 'Well?'

"La Pascalieri replied: 'Do you know Harriman?'

"'Obviously,' he said. ' Who doesn't know the
American billionaire whose arrival in Europe all the
newspapers announced last week? I'm certainly flattered
and happy on your behalf for such homage,'

"'Pardon me, but it isn't me that that voyage interests.'

"'What?'

"'Truly, my dear director, you don't know that
when he comes here, he gambles for high stakes and los-
es heavily?'

"'He can afford it,'

"'With what conviction you said that?' said La
Pascalieri, laughing.

"The director looked at her, and he smiled too. He
reread the telegram, handed it back to her and then rang.

"A few moments after that dialogue the artiste took
her leave, having exchanged her old contract for a new
engagement, in which the figure of her fee was doubled.
Now, do you know, Faxton, who sent that telegram?"

"Wasn't it Harriman?"

"No—and this is what demonstrates the excellence
of your apparatus: it was the interior laughter of La
Pascalieri, her intimate and amused thoughts, that revealed the underside of the affair to me.

"Thus, I learned that the sender was La Pascalieri's
man of confidence, who had remained in Paris on her
order expressly for that task. The artiste had learned before leaving of Harriman's intention of coming to Spa
today. Taking advantage of that coincidence, she had
immediately imagined, in concert with her factotum, the

ploy of the telegram, which, as you see, succeeded completely."

"That story, Jim, doubtless offers some interest, but it's my turn to declare that it doesn't seem very moral."

"Don't you think, Faxton, that these games that exploit the weakness of certain impassioned or rich idlers ought to be regarded as more moral? In sum, La Pascalieri creates beauty!"

"That's not an excuse."

"Perhaps not. Nevertheless, in this instance, what's important is that your machine works, and doubtless better than you hoped."

I only replied to Jim that, indeed, it was not in that fashion that I had wanted to inaugurate my apparatus.

Furthermore, those words reminded me that it was necessary to check whether La Pascalieri really was in Spa, the material details, such as her presence at ten past eleven in the office of the director of the Casino, and then to establish what had caused the range between Ostend and Spa, which singularly surprised my anticipations, since I had prepared for a transmission over a very short distance...

...We have spent two days in various trials, which I have noted down in the part of this notebook reserved for technical details. Jim lent himself with a good grace to those experiments, although they were fatiguing.

I was surprised by that, and I believe that it is necessary to attribute his complaisance to a motive other that scientific interest or even simply interest. I am absolutely convinced that what is leading him cannot by the hope of finding a definitive solution to the curious problem of telepathy.

As for his old fears, he has been able to convince himself of their inanity; he knows very well now that he has never been mad, nor on the point of becoming so. Nor does he intend to profit from state secrets to play the stock market, or attract public attention to himself and thus obtain some notoriety. Gambling doesn't seduce him, even on an almost sure thing. Furthermore, he is modest; the amplitude of a visible role on the world stage, celebrity and glory, no longer attract him.

Now, he brings to our work as much joy and enthusiasm as me, passionate for this research and the powerful emotions I owe to it. I can't believe that the amity he has for me, on its own, is sufficient to justify the vehemence of his good will. Let's hope, nevertheless, that his good dispositions don't abandon him too quickly...

...The tuning is improved.

...I believe that I 've discovered the reasons for Jim's extreme complaisance in my regard and his gaiety. They put on a rather pleasant feminine appearance, that of our gracious hostess. Really, Jim is in love; although he hasn't made me any confidence on that subject, and I'm too discreet to provoke any, it's impossible for me to conserve the slightest doubt. His precautions to hide that nascent sentiment from me, his attitudes and the inflections of his voice as much as his silences, all reveal the secret that he is trying to hide.

In truth, it required our voyage to the continent to produce that revolution in the fellow, for a few months ago, still, he did not seem to suspect that there existed in the world—apart from his sister Mary, for whom his affection is very limited—individuals other than masculine, and, by virtue of that fact, endowed with the different properties at which he now marvels to remark: discoveries compared with which those due to my games with lenses lose their value. It is thus that he has learned the precious savor that is conferred on a banal phrase by the mouth that pronounces it, the charm of a gaze, the attraction of a gesture or a smile, and the enchantment of a presence.

With small steps, delighted and astonished, he is penetrating into an unknown world, new for him, so different from the old one—which was solely populated by clients, colleagues and clerks, tumultuous, filled with din and telephone calls, the cries of brokers and agents—that he must not know exactly "whether he's dreaming or awake," as they sing in old ballads.

Poor Jim!

In spite of his physique—he has beautiful eyes, though—he is visibly seeking to please. He cares for his appearance and his French. The mystery of our sessions in the laboratory surrounds him with a sort of prestige, of which he makes much. I think that explains his assiduity and his enthusiasm. Perhaps he also adds to it the desire not to be far away from his beloved, sometimes to hear the sound of her footsteps in the garden, and her voice when she speaks to Rosa. Already, long conversations are being added to our meals, in the course of which he forgets me gladly.

VII. The Château de M***
(Continuation of Judge's Journal)

...I've succeeded, now, on the one hand, in eliminating the multiple influences that trouble the reception periodically, and on the other, in establishing a regular communication either at short or long distance.

In the latter category, I stopped at a château in the French Ardennes, for the strangeness of thoughts and impressions surprises determined us to pursue that curious observation uniquely, all the more facile as my apparatus continues to function marvelously.

I have been able to determine rigorously the position of the domain on the map and identify its owner, by consulting a directory, unknown to Jim. That check evidently remains in the general order, but it suffices for the moment, given the special character of the conversations heard, the ideas emitted and the décor seen. It will be easy for me, in fact, to complete my verifications later by a visit to the location.

In any case, I have no more reason for doubt since this morning; I recommenced my first trial with the aid of the translation of Dickens, and thanks to the recent improvement of the tuning, it succeeded.

I shall therefore summarize here, in the form of a running narration, what I have learned from Jim in recent days about Joseph L***, the owner of the property of M***, where he lives in retirement with a comrade, Georges V***, for it would be tedious to reproduce integrally and in the order in which I discovered them, the images from which I have reconstructed the appearance of places, remembrances, reflections and sensations that permitted me, as Jim's r evelations accum ulated, to r e-constitute the individuality of the principal actor, as well as that of his c onfidant—in sum, the totality of the d ia-logues between those two individuals.

Joseph L *** is a f ormer engineer, whose m odest origin forced h im t o s eek r emunerative e mployment a s soon as he obtained his diplomas. It is thus that, having equipped lines all over, and installed rails and trolleys in numerous cities in this native land, which was France, he had been led to e xpatriate himself, first to Egypt and then to less favored regions. Most recently, he had suc-ceeded i n di recting t he exploitation o f a tram-line in South A frica, w hen t he sudden decease o f a n unc le whose direct posterity had become extinct not long be-fore in consequence of malady and various accidents, put him in possession of a heritage as unexpected as it was considerable, which permitted him to hand in his resig-nation.

The f ortune t hat ha d be en t ransmitted to hi m in such a brutal fashion attained a volume sufficient for no breach to be made in it by a few months of follies, in the course o f w hich L *** materialized, in several con crete aspects, the dr eams t hat e very young a nd he althy i ndi-vidual c ultivates w ithin himself. In a r elatively sh ort time how ever, he knew the s pecial p overty of the rich, outside of af fairs, whose w ishes are too easily satisfied and t hus qu ickly c ut s hort desire a nd i magination. That life of opu lent i dleness requires a pr eparation t hat he lacked. The m etamorphosis t hat he h ad unde rgone h ad only transformed his social figure without endowing his mental pe rson or his phy sique w ith the sam e capa cities for expenditure.

Joseph L*** lived detestable days and worse nights. Only the habitudes of hygiene that he had brought back from his sojourn in the equatorial regions saved him from neurasthenia. He got away with a few weeks of shrill pessimism, which perhaps accentuated the stomach aches, headaches and other troubles left by the ingestion of port, bottles of extra-dry, fine and extremely respectable, that accompanied suppers offered to comrades to celebrated worthily the promotion of the engineer to the grade of multimillionaire in the capitalist class.

Only owing that favor to chance, Joseph L*** had not taken any pride from it. His natural modesty had thus preserved him from acquiring the state of mind common to the majority of parvenus, even intelligent ones, who cannot succeed entirely in masking their pride in having succeeded, their correlative scorn for the humble, their disdain for the semi-rich or the unlucky, their vanity unconsciously satisfied by all flatteries, including the most vulgar, irritated by the slightest lack of admiration, whence comes their tendency only to surround themselves with docile creature, subservient souls skillful in praising the master and basely sparing him criticism.

In addition, he did not experience any need to increase his income, which he already judged to be excessive, by employing his activity, doubled by his capital, in works of industry or commerce. Possession of a racing stable, a costly mistress and holding banks at baccarat did not tempt him at all. His tastes also distanced him from philanthropy, either laic or religious, from politics, and the mania of collecting art-works, occupations reputedly more moral than the aforementioned, and which aid with habitude those who deliver themselves to transforming into honors an excess of profits or income.

What should he do?

It was in that epoch that he thought about marriage, encouraged by a few excellent aged individuals among his relatives, who invited him to enlace their younger relatives and the daughters of their friends to the sound of exquisite music.

Doubtless he did not possess romantic dispositions, although in France, I am told, he was rather constrained and artificial in such matters. At any rate he was far from being seduced by the poetry of those balls, the innocence of the dancers; that engineer, probably being too materialistic did not obtain any pleasure therefrom. The noise of the orchestra, the savage fury of gypsies, the excess of flowers, perfumes, amiabilities, the turbulence of bright colors and the champagne sickened him.

The smiles of virgins appeared to him to be similar to those he knew already. Their eyes shone, like the others. The young man, not ugly but an "exceptional match" in the vocabulary of the good ladies who occupied themselves with finding him a twin soul, experienced the dread of not being selected for his own merits; whatever the personal fortune of the partners were proposed to him, he could not defend himself from the conviction that the poor were only accepting him for his money, and that, without that money, the rich would have refused him.

I suppose nevertheless that that slightly naïve judgment would easily have been modified if he had encountered some beauty susceptible of inspiring him, for want of real passion, merely with a strong inclination. But it is probable that none of his dancing partners succeeded in provoking a sentiment of that sort in him and that, at the same time, the amity of Georges V*** aided him to console himself intellectually for his matrimonial disillusionments.

Joseph L *** resigned himself, therefore, to living as a bachelor, as luxuriously as he had to. He bought the property of M***, and remodeled the château, hothouses and outbuildings in accord with his tastes. Then, gripped by nostalgia for his former métier, he had new buildings constructed, which he fitted out appropriately.

Those laboratories, with their library, their storerooms and their studio annexes, formed a kind of long glazed gallery backed up against a wall and overlooking a delightful corner of the park, where clumps of maples and bamboos were reflected in a small pond, putting in the hollow of a lawn the bright patch of its water, crowned with arums and ne nuphars. Further away, clumps of bushes disposed in a semicircle circled the curve of a pathway shaded by chestnut trees. Beeches and aspens succeeded them, leading toward the hothouses.

Monumental, their fragile architecture loomed up at the edge of the forest where, on August afternoons, between the blades of the blinds, a thousand rays of flamboyant sunlight, refracted by the glass, launched in high curves toward long narrow platforms flanking a central cupola. The dome sheltered a vast rotunda paved with marble, around which naiads pursued by fauns and tritons mingled their metal hair with the corollas of nympheas and lotuses enameling pools, basins and fountains, which flowed over the lace of mosses and aquatic plants. Arborescent ferns from Australia, coconut palms and banyans dominated their groups. A statue by Rodin stood in the center, springing from a flower-bed of orchids. Behind it, the mosaics of a stairway with a double revolution formed a singular tapestry, which garlanded the wrought iron balustrades all the way to the circular balcony s upported by l ight c olonnettes, w hich almost disappeared under the delicate guipure of lianas.

Through hi gh t win po rches, the la teral g alleries opened t heir b ronze doors ornamented w ith h aut-reliefs to t he i nterior of the i mmense ha ll. T hey poured out a perpetual lukewarm flux of odors, uniting the aromas of distant sp ices w ith t he p erfumes of ex otic o r familiar fruits, the e ffluvia of s oils, r esins a nd f lowers. P lants, each in its native humus, the rarest individuals of vegetal races sca ttered over t he s urface of the g lobe, had been brought together there. To the right were the Asiatic and American galleries, to the left the African and Oceanian. Indigenous gardeners car ed for cer tain species of t heir native l ands t here. To the J apanese, however, was re- served not on ly the pr uning of c entenarian dwarf trees, minuscule v egetations or namenting cer tain rocks t hat simulated miniature mountains, with their roads, bridges, temples and precipices, disseminated within the gallery, but also the m aintenance o f ba skets su spended more or less everywhere and bouquets placed on the tables of the rotunda, c omposed i n a ccordance with the r ules of t he special art that is taught in the Empire of the Rising Sun.

By ni ght, no l amp w as lit, bu t t he w aters o f t he fountains, ha ving be come l uminous, s ufficed, by means of their v ariously c olored surfaces, to illuminate with a spray of v arious radiances, harmonious, m elting a nd soft, the g lass v essels sh eltering t he silent life o f the plants.

When Jim described these splendors to me and the admiration superimposed in him by J oseph L ***'s own sensations, I e xperienced a v iolent e motion, a nd t hen a sort of jealousy that, in spite of all reason, urged me to- ward t he e nd of h is n arration to pu t on t he he lmet a nd use the apparatus to visit in my turn that palace of enchantments worthy of a caliph in the Arabian Nights.

And as a justification of my action, initially almost irreflective, I thought: *After all, without my apparatus, Jim wouldn't seem here or sense anything. Why should my play of lenses not be sufficient in itself to permit entering into communication with other brains?*

The conformation of my cranium, completely different from that of Double-Head, did not permit me an exact application of the principal skull-cap. In spite of my efforts to remedy that fault, which destroyed the necessary concordance between the focal points of the lenses, I only succeeded, once the fit had been perfectly obtained, in experiencing a frightful disappointment. It increased when I observed that my envious impulse had had even more unfortunate results: the loss of the reference-points carefully established to Jim's measurements and two crowns of brass, irremediably falsified. I possessed spare parts, it is true; nevertheless, I had to devote an entire morning to repairs and a new adjustment before rediscovering the residents of the Château de M***.

I recognized that that my first hypothesis was accurate. The success of our experiments depended, as I had supposed at first, not only on my ingenuity as a constructor, but above all on the exceptional properties of Jim's cranium and encephalum.

Thus far I have only spoken incidentally a but Georges V***, Joseph L***'s companion in his luxurious retreat. It is necessary for me to return to him.

He was an unlucky college friend whom the millionaire had found on his return to France, an engineer like him but reduced to sordid tasks. The poor fellow had reason to be satisfied with that encounter or multiple reasons; his comrade had assured him immediately of an unhoped-for position, associating him with his endeavors, and, being neither stupid nor a parvenu, as I have already noted, he consequently brought an extreme tact and delicacy to his relationship with Georges V***.

The later constituted a rather singular specimen of humankind. His intelligence and his skepticism had distanced him from all ambition, which likened him to the owner of M ***. Furthermore, a quasi-morbid fear of enslavement had never permitted him to retain a stable position; it was sufficient for him to be obliged to be present at a given time for him to experience a malaise, sometimes going as far as preventing him from going to the factory; an order provoked in him the unhealthy desire to execute it inversely; a task imposed on him inspired a repugnance, often difficult to vanquish, with the result that he had generally been held to be incapable, idle and unintelligent. With Joseph L***, who knew him and left him a complete independence, he gave proof, on the contrary, of remarkable qualities.

When the millionaire had explained to him the goal of his research, which was to verify whether the grimoires of the ancient alchemists—of which he has assembled an important collection, thanks to the interested zeal of a competent book-dealer—might contain glimpsed verities or approximations. He hastened to draw up a methodical plan of study, to translate into modern formulae the baroque recipes, to exclude, select, and finally, after copious eliminations, to submit to the approval of his comrade a method of transmutation found in a manuscript notebook of the late seventeenth century. The owner of M*** adopted it.

It was not a matter, of course, of reconstituting some ancient apparatus. Georges V*** had imagined a transposition, utilizing modern instruments and the most recent energy-sources. There again he exhibited an efficacious skill that could be exercised even in the organization of the smallest details of that strange experiment.

After the preceding, it will be easily understood that Jim's confidences regarding the singular inhabitants of that château in the Ardennes had incited me to maintain communication with them carefully, without seeking other correspondents for the moment. Jim was passionately interested himself in that multiple, romantic life, so different from our former communal existence in the Saint Barnaby Building and his visits to Mansur Cottage or to old Sam Lane. He did not raise any objections relative to the morality of those quotidian excursions in the domains and brains of others. I could measure his pleasure by the warmth of his reports.

At the same time, I ought to recognize that his character is not alone in being modified, and I should mention that a strange material transfiguration, if I might put it thus, had been operated in him. In the beginning, I had attributed that change, initially very slight, to the fortunate influence of the revelation of a sentimental life, previously unknown to him, which he owed to Madame Lansaert, about which I have already spoken. It happens, in fact, that on the occasion of an excitation of that sort, ugly men sometimes put on, in the presence of a woman they love, or even merely desire, a fleeting mask less displeasing than their habitual physiognomy, if not entirely handsome. The eyes open wider, shining with a more vivacious gleam; the features harmonize with the amiable discourse that the mouth pronounces, and which leads them to smile rather than grimacing. But in Jim's case, it seemed to me that something more must be intervening.

That simple enunciation offers, I am aware, such a contradiction with what anthropologists tell us about the fixity of types and races, and also with anatomical treatises of the subject of the human skeleton, that I hesitate, as soon as having formulated it, to complete my thought in that regard. In any case, rather than 'my thought,' it is 'my intuition' that it is necessary to write. On reflection, a first suspicion of that nature was born during the communication with La Pascalieri; on entering unexpectedly into the room where Jim retained an attitude, inexplicable for me at that moment, I had seen him clearly *other*. Then I had forgotten that necessarily brief impression.

Now I recall, in the same order of ideas, the strange sound of his voice, suddenly transformed, the unexpected modulations that had surprised me on that Saturday evening in London, at my house, when he had explained me so tranquilly that "the stones that burn" was a expression employed in a story of "his homeland," a "traveler's tale."

Evidently, an actor easily creates on stage a character somewhat different from his own corporeal existence. He curbs voluntarily to the measure of that artificial being his statue and his step, the inflection of his voice, and so on. Nevertheless, it is undeniable that Jim had never wanted to play a role, and had no thought of so doing, nor of composing a new physical appearance. He would not succeed, moreover, in that measure, for while becoming other, he remains natural.

Now, I am convinced that I am not duped by an illusion. Scarcely an hour ago, old Rosa confided to me, in a joyful tone, in designating Jim to me, who was accompanying Madame Lansaert in her visit to the garden:

"You know, Monsieur Judge, your friend seems to be profiting from being here. One wouldn't believe that he's the same fellow as when you arrived!"

IX. The Philosopher's Stone

This afternoon in August, at the Château de M***, facing the laboratories, the lawn and the pond, the verdure was ornamented by varied and changing colorations. Storm clouds, punctured by the sun, were marbling them alternately with light and shadow as they passed rapidly over the blue of the sky, sometimes veiled and sometimes resplendent.

Joseph L***, all engineer as he was, nevertheless retained a nature sensitive to that décor. The spectacle that it offered to him as that moment by virtue of the mobile play of its aspects attracted him enough to distract him from his work. Sitting on a stool placed in front of a shelf of varnished porcelain that ran along the panes of glass, he was watching through an open bay the flight of great somber patches. Pensive and motionless, he was silent.

Nearby, his comrade was smoking a cigarette.

They were both dressed in a bizarre costume, due to the invention of Georges V***, who had imagined the garment in question, simultaneously a conductor of electricity for a discharge caused by an awkward contact, and isolating its wearer. That special diving suit of sorts permitted a diver to plunge into the bosom of the most dangerous waves and handle them without dread.

There was a distant rumble of thunder.

The château-owner's collaborator, indicating the landscape, which a squall was animating with a tumult of noisy leaves, plaintive branches and rippled waters, said: " It would be prudent to close the windows; the storm is getting closer."

"Bah!" said the millionaire alchemist. "The build-ing is protected by lightning conductors, and as for us..." He indicated their accoutrement.

Georges V*** did not insist. He threw away what remained of the cigarette that he had just smoked, chose another from a packet placed between the test-tubes and the round flasks, rolled it mechanically between his fingers, gloved in gutta-percha, and then lit it at the flame of a gas-jet that was burning weakly under a hood at the back of the room.

"Let's go!" he said. "Are you coming with me to take the readings of our instruments?"

"No," replied Joseph L***. "Wait a moment; I don't feel well. Is it the enervating effect of this heavy weather? I don't know, but I'm experiencing a vague anguish."

"You're afraid. What have you to fear?"

"Do I know, exactly? Perhaps of succeeding! I was thinking that if, by a singular irony, this unusual power were given to me, who had already showed myself un-skillful at disposing of a relatively minimal quantity of this force, I'd find myself very embarrassed. What would I do with projection powder? What use would it be to me to be able to change tons of sand or lead into gold? I'm not even capable of spending all my income. Remember that my stomach imposes sobriety, that my heart forbids me the violet emotions of amour, gambling, politics and the automobile, and that my esthetics adapts poorly to anything but simplicity. It would be ridicu-lous!"

"But you're forgetting that it's not only a matter of that. We want to take matter at the emergence from the primitive womb and dress it as we please—in gold, if wish! Success... Sapristi! Success would make us the equal of gods, and the vulgar image of gold would fade away before the august grandeur of such a result. From a theoretical viewpoint, think..."

"I'm envisaging the practical app lications, and that's what frightens me."

"What! W ith a g esture, you'll a ccomplish w hat prophets, philosophers and revolutions have never been able to achieve! With a word, you'll undermine the barriers that the cen turies h ave not b een ab le to shake, which s ort m en i nto e nemy he rds, di vide them int o castes in the cr adle and maintain them separate until death! And that gesture and that word frighten you?"

"Miracles ha ve al ready be en worked. Whether i t produces new means of defense against diseases, or substitutes for the inadequacy of our organs by endowing us with artificial eyes, ears and legs, or c reates m achines untiringly, insensible and powerful beasts of burden, or scrupulous and adroit se rvants, science never c eases to accomplish t hem. They've onl y ev er con solidated t he barriers of which you speak.

"When mystical miracles are discovered positively, one caste, as you put it, takes possession of them at birth and carefully reserves the property and usage of the profits for itself, in order to maintain the slavery of t he others, who continue to envy the prerogatives and pleasures of t he former, and attempt t o substitute t hemselves for them. If t hey suc ceed, they r eveal t hemselves t o be harsher, more scornful an d more avaricious than their former masters. They don't break the barriers either—on the contrary!"

"Don't c ompare our w ork with what has been; examples are lacking in the history of the world. Tyrants have be en killed, kings guillotined, free peoples enchained, but who, over the centuries, has dared to touch gold? At present it is the sole monarch that truly reigns. It has always been the Omnipotent, the one on which empires depend and which divides between its innumerable subjects, favor or disgrace, joy or torture, the one that guards the triple rampart of laws, armies and mores. If we succeed, it will become a slave again. The crowds will be liberated from its domination and their servitude. At the same stroke, we'll free the creatures who are overwhelmed by excessively hard labor and the beings brutalized by excessive idleness, who lead a vile, incomplete, fallen existence. The fictions that guarantee its value will disappear."

"Others will be created. Will they be any better than the old ones? If humans had been able to replace gold with something better, wouldn't they have suppressed it already? People always talk about its misdeeds. You seem to believe, Georges, that it constitutes the great obstacle, against which humanity bumps and stops, in a hypothetical monarch toward a happier future. But think, if religions disappeared, if empires and emperors disappeared, and gold remained, wouldn't an indestructible necessity confer more eternity on it than religions, more power than empires, emperors and gods possess?

"In reality, it maintains the strength of nations in passing from one individual to another, in the fashion of the blood that aliments our body in flowing from cell to cell. Because anemia and congestion both constitute redoubtable diseases, is it necessary to conclude that it would be better to open the veins than to continue to suffer the tyranny of blood?

"Yes, I'm afraid of launching upon the world an infinite possibility of catastrophes. Fortunately, nothing permits us yet to foresee success."

There were a few moments of silence.

Georges V***, certainly touched by his friend's arguments, reflected.

"Perhaps y ou're r ight," h e e nded up r ecognizing. "Gold i s the hum an t hought t hat ha s e xtracted us from the v oid, s ustains us a nd c onstantly di spenses l ife. The animals are unaware of it; for a dog, an ingot of yellow metal is worth less than a bone. Be reassured, then! Let's admit for a moment that the problem is resolved and that the excellent gentleman's formula has enabled us to obtain, in the magical egg, the philosopher's stone. I f fear that, in that case, we'll have as many difficulties in convincing our contemporaries..."

"I don't want to do that."

"…As he has already encountered."

"What's that?"

"The m anuscript i n our p ossession seems t o have been signed with a false name, for you'll recall that our research into the C hevalier de V ersepleure w ere un able to furnish us with the s lightest information. No armorial mentions the title in question, probably a symbolic pseudonym. But the person who wrote that notebook, on the first page of which the signature forms that ironic mask, existed. Now, history has not registered his name."

"Doubtless he failed."

"You know that he claims the contrary, and lists the complicated p recautions he t ook t o avoid s uspicion. However, a secret is hard to keep. It's a t erribly st rong perfume, which is divined even when the bottle containing i t i s h ermetically sea led. That m an certainly p ossessed friends, a mistress, and valets. The truth, you see, is t hat i f y our pr oclaim t he d iscovery l oudly, y ou'll probably obtain a fleeting success of curiosity, without convincing anyone fundamentally, except alienist physicians, for whom you wouldn't be the first.

"I abandoned myself just now to an excessive lyricism as ill-founded as your fears, No, a gesture, a word, and facts serve for nothing in such matters. I was wrong, in fact, when I accused gold of cementing the walls that separate humans. The real barriers are ridges of thought, edified in the granite of instinct with the quarry-stone of sentiments and the mortar of habits. My hopes and your fears are dreams, chimeras, illusions! It would need a projection powder that could transmute the contents of brains. Manufacturing tons of gold wouldn't change the value of a word. Others would remain, of a superior value, since they'd gladly exchange their gold against those words..."

"Georges," said Joseph L*** then, " how disconcerting you are! Your speech is like those storm clouds, which contain enemy electricities and pursue one another impetuously, distributing so much shadow and so much light."

His comrade smiled and concluded: " That doesn't prevent me, from the moral and material viewpoints alike, from persisting and affirming that we're both mistaken, you in dramatizing your fears and me in magnifying my hopes. Come on! We can continue our work placidly, and succeed. We'll only change, if we're not taken for madmen, practical formulations, textbooks of chemistry and the metallurgical tools in a few factories..."

A series of formidable cracks interrupted him, while the sky lit up with a network of slender violet streaks.

Georges V*** went on: "Fine weather for playing Fausts!"

"Without Marguerite," observed Joseph L***.

"Yes, and perhaps that's better... In the meantime, I'm going to work!"

He he aded toward t he ne arby l aboratory. B efore crossing the threshold he put a ki nd of m ask w ith glass eyepieces over his face.

A r umble of thunder s pread its s onorous cascades. Large raindrops be gan to f all. An a erial t urbulence of moist odo rs and b roken twigs c ame t o l ash Joseph L***'s face; mechanically, he threw himself backwards and br ought dow n the v isor of h is he lmet i n hi s t urn. However, he did not follow his comrade.

Maintaining a w eary a nd m editative a ttitude, he gazed, without seeing them, at the maples, the bamboos and the plaintive shrubs curbed by the gusts of wind, the hasty ripples in the little pond, now stained by patches of tarnished bronze. In resonances of as sociation, hi s c ol-laborator's last words were prolonged in his mind: Mar-guerite, i nnocence, a mour… but a lso.. jewels! T he ol d poet h imself h ad only est eemed the be auty of the g en-tleman; his prestige his vigor, his rediscovered youth; the cu lture and subtlety of hi s i ntelligence w ere suf fi-cient to seduce Marguerite, but gold intervened: the irre-sistible conqueror, victorious gold, gold… forever!

X. The Interrupted Theft

The engineer's reflections led him to wonder whether the Chevalier de Versepleure really had obtained the definitive transmutation or some analogous result, because that passage in the manuscript remained frightfully obscure, doubtless by design, and almost untranslatable. It was with great difficulty, at any rate, that the two friends had been able to decipher the texts relative to the manual operation and the calculation of time. In that regard, he remembered abruptly that the duration of their manipulations corresponded, almost to the minute, with the term indicated by the alchemist. A vaguely anguished curiosity lifted him from his stool.

As he was about to go and rejoin Georges V** in the laboratory a second gust of wind projected a cloud of dust and water into the laboratory, bathed in the blinding reflections of a flash of lightning. Instead of being rapidly extinguished, however, the intensity of the unusual light was suddenly augmented, becoming similar to the radiation produced by the incandescence of a sheet of molten metal. At that moment, Joseph L*** heard confused exclamations in the next room, and at the same moment the crash of thunder, accompanied by such a recrudescence of light that he had to close his eyes.

When he opened them again, the first object that imposed itself on his gaze was a red sphere the size of an orange. It was moving slowly over the floor. Immediately, he thought that it must be ball lightning, and that it was about to burst, but that, fortunately, he was protected by the armor of his insulating garment. A round glass flask pl aced close by , on a t able, oscillated and then broke with a dry click. One of the table legs split.

Meanwhile, the ball rose up. After having described an incomplete spiral, it remained suspended in the air for a moment, seemed to head toward the open bay and the garden, a nd then s topped and de scended to t he g round again, without exploding, to the great amazement of Joseph L ***. F inally, a fter its c oloration h ad pa ssed to crimson, it became a sort of large iridescent soap bubble, which remained m otionless i n the m iddle of t he r oom, and then pivoted on itself, accel erated its m ovement of rotation m ore a nd m ore, a nd s lid w hile s pinning un der the po rcelain s helf running a long t he w indows, no t f ar from t he s eat f rom w hich the ow ner o f t he C hâteau de M*** had got up a few moments earlier. There, its sparkling colors were extinguished at it was confounded with the shadow.

Absorbed by the c ontemplation of the s trange ph enomenon, t he e ngineer di d not tr y t o i nterpret it . He strove in v ain to p enetrate the ob scurity, r endered m ore opaque at ground level. His heart was beating heavily in his c hest. H e w as c hoking. H owever he w as afraid of approaching the wall near to which the thing had disappeared; in spite of h is de sire to see it again, he w as a pprehensive of moving without knowing its cause. A stupid fear pa ralyzed hi m, pr eventing hi m f rom g oing t o find hi s comrade, d eforming t he v ision of f amiliar objects. The r oom, w hich he ha d not qui t a nd w here he dared no t budg e, seemed t o hi m t o b e full o f invisible dangers. He was dom inated by the a bsurd c ertainty that an unknown peril was menacing him, an enemy lurking in ambush that would not fail assail him if he risked an imprudent step or a maladroit gesture.

That bizarre emotion became so intense that he stifled an oath on perceiving that his insulating garment prevented him from drawing a revolver from the pocket of his trousers.

Why a revolver? Against whom? He found himself grotesque. But, stronger than his reason, the impression of terror subsisted. He did not linger over the argument. Only the possession of a weapon was important to him. By turns he examined the furnaces, the retorts, the hooks, and the iron supports, too f rail. Finally, he breathed out; under the hood, between the weakly-burning gas jet from which Georges V *** had lit his cigarette and a precision balance, enclosed in its cage of glass, lay a chisel for cutting metal, forgotten there, offering itself. While keeping watch on the place where the enigmatic apparition had disappeared, the engineer, overcoming his fear of any movement, headed for the saving object.

As soon as he had seized it in his gloved hand, he was unable to suppress a nervous laugh; a puerile joy invaded him at that facile triumph. The possession of the vulgar instrument restored his lost courage, bringing him security and deliverance. His previous terror seemed devoid of any object.

Having become braver, he decided to take account immediately of the presence or disappearance of the mysterious sphere. However, he could not resolve to let go of the chisel, which he had in his left hand. With the right he picked up a long glass rod, and commenced his exploration under the porcelain shelf, from the corner formed by the wall between the room and the garden and the one that separated the laboratory from the vestibule.

He only brought out flakes of dust, revealing nothing but the negligence of the cleaner, and was about to continue when he reflected that it would be preferable if Georges V*** helped in the research, so as to check on what would happen in the improbable case of a further event. He hailed his comrade.

The latter came, cursing. Doubtless as a consequence of the storm, the instruments had been out of kilter or a few minutes, most of the apparatus had ceased functioning; a great deal of work remained to do, and urgent work, under pain of seeing the "egg" cool down at the decisive moment, if he did not want to have to start all over again.

"Why that bizarre equipment?" he asked, only remarking then Joseph L ***'s attitude, staring into the shadow, armed with his rod and his chisel.

The other did not have time to respond.

In spite of the continued patter of raindrops rebounding from the windows and the roof of the gallery, the dull rumbles of thunder that continued to agitate the atmosphere, the racket of the wind whipping the treetops in the park, a different noise, nearer, reached their ears, strangely precise. Their masks did not succeeded in stifling the high-pitched vibrations, almost musical, because they succeeded one another in accordance with a regular, rhythmic, obsessive design covering about an octave and a half.

That singular music, which they heard clearly, emanated from the place opposite which Joseph L was standing. He knew that it must be the sphere that was emitting the sequence of sounds. He tried to explain it to his friend, to bring him up to date, but his thoughts scattered, without him being able to stop one and translate it into words. He could only extend the rod in the direction of the wall toward which the iridescent globe had headed before disappearing.

Georges V*** followed that gesture with his gaze and leaned over, only to get up almost immediately, crying out. He snatched the glass rod from his comrade's hands and drew successively to their feet a s topper, a fragment of a test-tube and an amorphous mass that must have been a tampon of cotton wadding.

It was then the turn of Georges V*** to howl; the cork, the broken glass and the wad of cotton, as they rolled over the floor of the laboratory, had produced a characteristic metallic sound. Not only did they appear uniformly yellow and shiny, but the engineer perceived now what had caused his collaborator's shock: reflections of gold gleamed beneath the porcelain shelf, dressing the plinth, the wall and the ground with the same glittering livery, over which the buzzing sphere could scarcely be distinguished by its fleeting contours, analogous to the vibration of the air when it is overheated by the burning days of high summer.

Alarmed, the two engineers recoiled instinctively. This was not how they had foreseen the denouement of the experiment, reconstituted in accordance with the Chevalier de Versepleure's manuscript. Instead of the delirious joy on which they had counted if they succeeded, these phenomena of transmutation, accomplished outside the "egg," uncatalogued and inexplicable, at least for the moment, disconcerted them, only procuring them a fearful surprise. Too intense and too sudden, their emotion remained more painful than agreeable, troubling those minds accustomed to the certainty of mathematical solutions, disciplined by the rigor of formulae, and reluctant to submit to the unusual vision, causing them and embarrassment that augmented, a malaise quickly increased to a frisson, before an incident whose rapid unfolding made them shiver with an equal effort.

A bee, chased by the storm, had entered, buzzing. It described a few crotchets, terminated by a winged curve, which ought to have brought it to that part of the floor where the magician globe was singing. It did not reach it, for, twenty centimeters before arriving there, it suddenly ceased flying and fell on to the tiles. For a fraction of a second its body quivered, its wings still agitating convulsively, and then stiffened. Rapidly then, an inexorable yellow tint metalized the insect.

By means of the glass rod, Georges V***, drew the tiny cadaver toward him and picked it up. Unable to help a slight nervous tremor, he held it out to his friend.

One might have thought it a jewel, marvelously sculpted in virgin gold, so clearly were the smallest fibers and most delicate stripes designed, all the details of the head, the thorax, the abdomen and the legs, stiffened without the slightest appearance of any substance foreign to the precious metal.

However, in spite of the revelatory weight of the insect, a doubt still held the mind of the engineer. He approached a box of reagents, and proceeded with a trial. It was decisive; the bee behaved like a gold ingot, chemically pure. Successively, the stopper, the fragment of the test-tube and the cotton wad gave identical results.

Those various manipulations, to which Joseph L*** had lent his collaboration, had only lasted a quarter of an hour. During that short space of time, the two friends had not quit the part of the laboratory opposite the window. When they had concluded the analysis, the accomplishment of the professional gestures that it necessitated, the manipulation of familiar instruments, the atmosphere itself saturated with accustomed vapors, the reek of acids, had appeased their souls.

Georges *** laughed childishly. "I think," he explained, "about what poor Père Schulz would have done, if he had seen that, who treated transmutation as a formidable stupidity and professed the same solid scorn for alchemists as for poets. It's true that he had a strange fashion of summarizing all of poetry in one distich. Do you remember?"

"Yes:

As the sun appears on the horizon.
Send me, father, a chorizo!

"He declaimed that puerile parody of lyricism in a grotesque tone, and every time it succeeded in provoking a noisy, naïve and satisfied hilarity in him..."

Gripped again by the present, however Joseph L*** continued:

"Do you really believe that the Chevalier de Versepleure, in possession of imperfect means, even more rudimentary knowledge, obtained the result that we..."

He hesitated, almost doubting, in spite of the evidence.

"...That we are forced to observe," completed his comrade, who went on: "I'm certain of it. In any case, a passage in his manuscript indicates it. By virtue of having reread it I know it by heart. We never succeeded in translating it in a manner to obtain a clear meaning from it. Now I can decipher it easily. It's this:

"*Remember that to the Sun has devolved in part the attributes of Venus and Mars. At the 441st hour fear the burning rays by which it announces its advent! If they ripen the crops and promise abundant harvests, they become as dangerous and as deadly for the madman* *who exposes himself imprudently to their inflamed darts as they remain beneficent and salutary for the sage who welcomes them without reserve.*"

"Which signifies…?"

"That he was less surprised than us. He was not unaware that t he S un p articipates in bo th V enus a nd Mars—which is to say that Gold contains the principles of Air and Fire. In consequence, it would have appeared normal to him that the composite of Air and Fire, before its definitive sol idification, 'announces i ts advent' by a radiation, on the subject of which he gives his advice of prudence. The example of the bee shows superabundantly that there is indeed reason 'at the 441st hour...'"

"The time is exact."

"…To f ear t he ' burning r ays,' e ven t hough t hey 'ripen the crops,' a self-explanatory image that alludes to the op eration of transmutation, 'promising a bundant harvests," w hich renders them ' beneficent and salutary for the sage.' But..."

"What?"

"The music has finished. Our egg is probably commencing to cool down."

Georges V*** was about to launch himself toward the po rcelain s helf unde r which t he y ellow reflections persisted when his comrade stopped him, seizing him so forcefully by the arm that Georges V*** cried out i n pain.

"Are y ou forgetting t he C hevalier's r ecommendations?" said Joseph L***. "Look!"

He poi nted a t the t able t hat t he engineer h ad b een about t o g o a round, w hich s eparated them f rom t he glazed bay. A brilliant dusting of red tending to carmine was creeping there, climbing up the crystal of the broken flask, the transparency of which was gradually diminishing, replaced by a crimson tint that darkened gradually, becoming opaque violet, almost black, and then yellow.

The two men then sensed a merciless fear invade them; it swelled the beating of their hearts in their breasts, plunged a red-hot iron into their throats and stuck their tongues to their desiccated palates. For at present, the storm had fallen silent. A few drops of water were falling from the calm leaves on to the gravel of the paths. They could only hear that slight sound; they could no longer distinguish the imprecise vibrations that had informed them a little while ago of the presence of the sphere, then buzzing. Only the transmutation of objects in the zone attained by the invisible emanations of the mysterious globe warned the two friends of its existence, and reminded them that it had lost nothing, in that new state, of its former power, a dangerous, frightening menace, specified terribly in their eyes by the minuscule cadaver of the golden bee and the memory of its interrupted flight.

It was no longer a matter of social dreams, discussions of hypotheses and exchanges of anticipations. Realty imposed itself, far more menacing. What defense had they to oppose to the brutality of facts?

All their science, found wanting, their past of study and labor, was turned upside down by that formidable unexpected event; even their imagination, caught short, only served to confirm their retched impotence, augmenting their weakness, their disturbance and their peril at the present moment.

Instinct, surviving in them for want of reason, reacted abruptly; without exchanging a word, the two men, with an almost automatic movement, slid along the mass of masonry occupying a part of the laboratory, supporting gas burners and the equipment with which they carried out their analyses. They went around it all the way to the back of the room, where they plastered themselves against the wall, unable to flee any further.

Huddled in that retreat, pressed together, in silence, they gazed fearfully at the infernal table, now a little further away from them. Only a vague sparkle could be discerned there, a play of nuances, idle changes in coloration, but their alert minds transformed the tranquil charm of the spectacle into a motif of terror and horror.

Time passed. The red dusting had continued its progress, and behind it, two-thirds of the table had already acquired the definitive yellow adornment.

Then Georges V*** was the first to decide to speak. He did so in a hoarse voice that his friend did not recognize. He did not turn his head and his comrade listened in the same attitude.

"It's necessary to do something," he pronounced, with difficulty, "and above all... not to stay here for too long...for if it continues its advance...we risk being stupidly blockaded, and... and then... it wouldn't be for long!"

At those words, Joseph L*** made an irrational gesture; he started feeling the wall behind him feverishly, as if to assure himself that it was still there, smooth and implacable, and had not opened up. In their course, his fingers bumped into the packet of dusty glass rods standing in the corner, from which he had borrowed the one he had used to explore the underside of the shelf before Georges V*** had snatched it away from him. That contact unleashed in his mind a rapid series of associations of ideas, which he expressed.

"First, it's necessary to k now. It might have changed form, for suppose that the vapor..."

"What vapor?" Georges V*** interrogated.

"Vapor… vibration… whatever you wish. I mean the matter, or the particular state of matter, represented by that sphere. Suppose, then, that instead of being condensed under that aspect of a globe, which we both recognized, that vapor... that vibration... in sum, that X, being extended, continues to disintegrate, or only to move irregularly, given that now it remains invisible, what assurance do we possess that of not encountering it unexpectedly, and being struck exactly where we believed ourselves to be most secure? Whereas by not budging…creating, for example, a sort of barrage with pieces of furnaces and glass tubes in a palisade…"

George V*** shrugged his shoulders and, striking the mass of masonry with his fist, he howled: "Sapristi! Don't you see that in a quarter of an hour, it, or its radiation, has come from the plinth under the window to that table, that it has scaled it, that in another quarter of an hour, it has metalized two-thirds of it? Where will it be before we've had time to make that barrage? And what barrage? How will we render it impermeable, since it traverses solid bodies in transforming them?"

Joseph L*** sighed. "What are we going to do?"

"Come what may," said his comrade, "I don't want to die in this corner like a rat. That would be too stupid! Stay if you want to. I'm going to try to get out."

"Georges! Don't do anything foolish! Wait!"

"Wait for what?"

"A new change of state, a modification…perhaps inoffensive this time…"

"Or more dangerous. Thank you very much! I prefer to climb over the furnace and try to get away, while there's still time. I estimate that to the left of the table, the space between it and the wall is sufficient for me to be able to pass through it rapidly."

"I beg you, don't leave me."

"Well, come with me."

"No, I can't! I'm afraid. Listen, Georges, listen to me! Yes, you're right; the palisade of glass tubes is absurd. It has attacked the broken flask on the table. But they might be of use to us."

"How?"

"Precisely because they'll react like the flask. They're two meters long. Take these, lay them down in front of the furnace, keep a few, which you can hold in a bouquet, scattered, held at the height of your chest. I'll do as much in front of me, and we'll thus know very quickly what the limits are of the expansion of the vapor; the change of coloration will inform us, without danger. Do you understand? Without danger!"

This time, Georges V*** obeyed without argument. The sheaves extended rigidly, forming a double fan that oscillated between the clenched hands of the two men.

A minute went by, reassuringly. The extremities of the twin sprays, like the rods placed on the laboratory floor, had not lost the gray velvet with which the dust enveloped the reflections of crystal.

A sigh escaped from Joseph L***'s breast. A joyful release constrained Georges V*** to laugh. They dared to turn their gazes toward the golden table and their apparatus of information. Georges V*** the perceived the face of Joseph L*** with the same joy that the latter received on seeing the face of his comrade again. An infinite peace, a rare sentiment of happiness filled their hearts with delight.

Gradually, a common desire for action came to them, which was translated initially because they no longer feared speaking. They exchanged the cries of schoolboys after class, banal and amused replies, empty words but num erous, f or the pl easure of h earing t heir voices r esound a gain in t he s onorous room, ha ving b e-come natural again, freed from accents of folly or terror.

Then they e mbraced, a nd ut ilized t he long t ubes like exploratory antennae. Georges V*** slid in front of the m ass of m asonry, r eached w ithout encumbrance the portion perpendicular t o the furnace, a nd be gan to e dge along it, stopping prudently from time to time to observe the ex tremities of t he g lass r ods, serving as w itnesses, while his comrade maneuvered in the same fashion, with his back against the opposite wall

To their g reat s urprise, they a rrived, e ach w ithout encumbrance, at a lmost the sam e t ime, one at t he do or, left ope n, to t he r oom w here the a pparatus h ad be en knocked over by the storm and the escape of the egg, the other at the frame of the one that gave access to a vesti-bule communicating with the garden.

The certainty of t heir d eliverance co nferred a ne w audacity on t hem. T hey attempted to join up a gain, em-ploying t he p recautions w ith w hich they w ere n ow f a-miliar, and s ucceeded in shaking ha nds, w ith a pa ssion-ate grip, the middle of the laboratory.

Without t he irreducible p roof of fered, by i ts m agi-cal as pect, by t he g old table cl ose t o which, still em o-tional and a stonished, they f ound themselves al ive, they would ha ve be en inclined t o de ny t he r ecent p ast; the vision of t he buz zing s phere, t he de ath o f t he be e, t he knell of the raindrops s ounding lugubriously in place of the m usic o f the m ysterious g lobe a fter the trial of the metalized objects, and finally the la st transmutation of the modest oak item of furniture.

Dazzling, t hey of fered t hus a m arvelous w ork of sculpture, in which the slightest veins of wood, respected in t heir de sign, t raced a c urious pa ttern, attenuating by frail fringes of shadow the glare of the excessively new metal. They lifted it up with great difficulty. As it fell back it resonated like a bell, spreading vibrations of an adorable purity, which sang for a long time, filling the entire being of the two friends with superstitious alarms before the mystery, even though they had summoned it, but also with a joy of conquerors after a victory, for they had touched that virgin gold with their creative hands. Soon, no dread any longer restrained the happy delirium that invaded them.

However, Joseph L*** began to go pale; his fatigued heart had received a series of excessively violent shocks from that succession of brutal emotions. The millionaire dissimulated his emotion under a mask of gaiety and said;

"Let's not stay here, old man! We'll try later to clarify all this. For the moment, I need air, a great deal of air, and also to see the trees again that are in the wood. Too much gold… there's too much gold here!"

Georges V*** smiled, without having remarked his friend's physical disturbance.

After having closed the door and shot the safety bolt that, when they desired, stopped the laboratory assistant from going into the two rooms, they rid themselves feverishly of their special costumes in the antechamber vestry. Finally, they went out hastily, in the fashion of someone escaping from a nightmare.

In the park, to the sway of the foliage varnished by the downpour, the blue of the sky seemed sometimes to diminish and sometimes to increase, inscribing mobile signs between the gaps. The green lances of the lawn darted diamond points at the sky. Birds chirped in the hollows of arbors. Clumps of flowers poured out a fresher and stronger perfume.

Three little w hite bu tterflies pur sued on e a nother over a pathway, and then disappeared behind a basket of roses.

XI. A Sentimental Crisis

A f ew seco nds a fter those ev ents in Ostend, Jim Broks, r egretfully qui tting M adame L ansaert, w ho ha d finished pruning the rose-bushes, rejoined F axton Judge in the studio. H is manner contrite and his eyes lowered, without a ny ot her pre amble, he s aid, s ighing: "My de ar friend, I owe you a confession."

"Hmm!" said Judge, who could not repress a smile, "If I'm not m istaken it's already som e t ime si nce y ou contracted that debt.

"Less than y ou t hink," r eplied J im, "for i t's onl y since half an hour ago that I've been aware of it."

"Poets and painters are right, then, to depict Amour with a blindfold over his eyes."

"What! Faxton, you've perceived..."

"That Madame Lansaert doesn't leave you indiffer-ent? Certainly! And since more than half an hour ago, I assure you."

"Then y ou'll e asily unde rstand t hat I must be v ery unhappy."

"This time, you surprise me. Your confidence I ex-pected f rom one da y t o t he ne xt, b ut r ather und er the form of c onfessions e nlivened by di thyrambs, hym ns and litanies, customary t o pe rsons w ho receive suc h a windfall. So, I c an't e xplain your reserve and your s ad-ness."

"Think, my good friend, that I love her, and... I'm ugly. I'm not una ware that I 'm i rredeemably ug ly. My dear Mary has taken care to inform me of that since my early c hildhood. A t that a ge, t he m emory r egisters the words of e lders i n a n a lmost i ndelible f ashion; s o my sister's lessons remain profoundly engraved in my head, my poor Double Head, and no longer permit me any illusion. To l ove, F axton, to love w ith m y ph ysique, doomed t o di sdain, rebuffs a nd m ockery—what no n-sense!

"At least, I st ill r easoned like t hat yesterday; I be-lieved myself to be p rotected by the s olidity of my judgment against a stupid error. But today, suddenly, the perfume of the flowers, mingled with hers, the brush of a wisp of h er ha ir ag ainst me che ek, the soft ness o f her voice and her gazes have informed me dolorously of the weakness, the v anity a nd t he ne gligibility of the b est logic i n these ci rcumstances. I 've unde rstood t hat o ne can't expel amour by reciting maxims and sentences, as one drives away and importunate wasp with a hand ges-ture or waving a napkin. It imposes itself whatever one does. It knocks y ou ov er without o ne being a ble to de-fend one self against the a ssault. It grabs you entirely, unexpectedly, m ore t reacherously t han a s hiver o f ma-lign fever.

"I'm very i ll! F axton, my dear phy sician, cure me again, I beg you."

"Amour isn't an i llness, Jim, and I've told you be-fore that I'm not a phy sician. On the other hand, you're forgetting t hat be auty of c haracter e xists, that a w oman is able to appreciate that beauty, and that intelligence..."

"Don't go on! Your generosity would like to con-sole m e. A las, m y D ouble-Head, m y s ickly body, a nd my di sgraceful appearance are seen first, and above all, and e verywhere. I n t he s treet, t hey a lone c ount. O ne doesn't walk around in spirit, and the most beautiful soul in the world would attract fewer gazes than a handsome fellow."

"But you don't care about passers-by, Jim; only the taste of a single woman matters to you. Thus far, that person doesn't seem displeased by your company. Really, I don't understand your despair."

"Unfortunately, Faxton, it's only too well-founded. Do I know, anyway, what sentiment inspires that condescension in accepting my company? Can you affirm to me yourself that it isn't it isn't simply an almost-commercial desire not to ill-dispose a client? I'm a guest, a boarder; in my case, I ought to dread and also to fear...pity."

"Why hold to the worst suppositions and take pleasure in torturing yourself, instead of simply admitting what doubtless risks approaching the truth, that someone finds some charm in your presence, your conversation, and can experience for you, if not amour, at least amity? Evidently, I'm not unaware that the majority of amorous individuals don't consent gladly to tolerating that the fury of their passion has no echo. It appears to them absolutely legitimate to demand a reciprocity of violence, otherwise..."

"Oh, I don't have so much ambition. But take account; it's necessary for me, contrary to your way of seeing, to worry about passers-by...of both sexes. If the situation in which I find myself seems miserable, without issue, it's because I only envisage with an insurmountable repulsion the prospect of inflicting upon a companion, whom I love and who loves me, the suffering that certain glances and certain smiles cause me. I'm habituated to it myself, since childhood...but she..."

Jim could not finish the sentence commenced. He collapsed in a chair, weeping silently.

This time, in spite of the emotion that he felt and his desire to console poor Jim, Judge found nothing to respond, only being surprised by having lived for such a long time beside his associate without having suspected in him the existence of that secret wound.

With regard to masculine ugliness, he had shared the generally admitted idea that esthetic considerations are only to be taken into consideration in the female sex, the "fair sex," whose prerogative they remain, moral qualities being sufficient for men. He perceived now the fragility of that conception, against the falsity of which Jim's dolor was inscribed. What refutation could be opposed to the all too legitimate arguments of the unfortunate lover? To tax his scruples with exaggeration would not suffice to suppress them.

Abruptly, Judge remember Rosa's words, confirming his own remarks. The hypothesis that, despite that observation he had refused to formulate in his notes, presented itself again, with an increased clarity and an irrefutable authority. It was no longer "intuition," as he had defined it, even less a "suspicion" of intuition, easily refuted by the contradiction that he had supposed at first between the data that he brought to the mass of those already acquired. Apart from the fact that, as a theory, it required numerous arguments, which did not shore it up in Judge's mind with rational support, from the practical and immediate point of view, it was fortified by a character of sentimental necessity, because it offered a miraculous means of exit from the impasse in which Jim had engaged.

It was not absurd, in sum, Judge thought, forgetting his initial objections, drawn from the fixity of the human skeleton and other considerations of that sort, inverting the comparison that had already served him, to suppose—following the example the actor whose face, body and gesture varied by mean of their mobile play of expression, deforming, remaking and modeling him in accordance with the sentiments whose representation had been confided to him—that Jim's physical mask, translating the thoughts of the owner of the Château de M   , might be subject to an analogous transformation, modified by the sort of mental transfusion that repeated telepathic communications operated every time in his brain.

No! In reality, neither Rosa nor he had been duped by a mirage; Jim had become other. Who could tell whether Madame Lansaert's inclination might have been motivated by the fortunate perturbation that had recently accomplished the difference in the physiognomy of the face and mannerisms that, although not very pronounced, nevertheless remained real.

Reverting from his former impressions, full of enthusiasm for that unexpected solution, prompt to admit what he had condemned, Judge gradually convinced himself that the phenomenon, in itself, looked at closely, did not contain anything inexplicable or surprising, if one considered that, from childhood to old age, our body and our mind are changing perpetually.

In certain individuals, no vestige subsists of what they were at a given period of their lives; a thin, plain girl can give birth to a pretty one; a hideous old woman might not recall in any fashion the admirable woman she once was; a tall, pale, handsome and pessimistic adolescent can become a fat, rubicund and self-satisfied man. Only memory, in them and others, attests that they have lived under a different appearance, so dissimilar to the one they have acquired over time that the fact, affirmed to those to people who did not know them before, would seem incredible.

As for the durable element, it also varies from one person to another and according to circumstances. An illness, a convalescence, a grave emotional or physical shock, will often suffice to aid rapidly either a decadence or a rebirth, a deterioration or a restoration of the features.

That series of deductions led Judge to examine his associate with minute attention.

One detail struck him immediately. The garments that Double-Head habitually wore very loosely, which usually floated around his thin limbs, fit him better. Indubitably, the drooping shoulders had straightened up, the chest was more rounded, adhering to the cloth. Afterwards, he observed that in the face, the hollow cheeks had been partly filled-in, which, combined with the previous remark, corresponded to the satisfied observation of the Flemish cook, attributing that plumpness to the excellence of her meals. In addition, the thinness of the lips, which lent them a grimacing appearance, had attenuated; the mouth had acquired a more amiable design in consequence. The brow ridges seemed less prominent. The bumps in the nose were fading. The hair had not retained its pale redness and was darkening toward chestnut.

Although they were not entirely unexpected, on registering the results of his inspection, Judge shivered, prey to brutal and contradictory emotions. Before that metamorphosis, which he could no longer put in doubt, he shuddered, receiving simultaneously a warm flush of joy caused by that enormous enlargement of his discovery, the vision of the therapeutic efficacy that it permitted it to apply in Jim's particular case, and a vague chill of terror, on thinking of the unknown that those lenses, that tripod and that apparatus contained, all the power of which he had not divined, and which now, an enigmatic sorcery, loomed up before him full of real promise and pregnant with mysterious threats. What more would emerge from it? Confusedly he feared a danger, which he could not specify.

Jim interrupted his reflections.

"Your silence, Faxton, informs me sufficiently," he said. "You think exactly as I do, don't you? You understand now that I'm not exaggerating in treating what has happened to me as a misfortune. Well, I think that the best thing for me to do is flee. That way, I'll doubtless forget; I hope that I'll finish up by forgetting. According to the French saying, 'far from the eyes, far from the heart.' Isn't absence, in such circumstances, the only remedy?"

He sighed, and then went on: "But will I have the strength? Promise to aid me in that! It's necessary, for, at the thought of leaving, of quitting her, of never seeing her again—never!—I remain devoid of courage and I believe that I'd prefer to continue suffering, and suffering more, by staying near her. Faxton, I swear to you that I no longer recognize myself. Who could have told me that I'd become so denuded of energy, so stupidly sentimental? Forgive me, my poor friend, I'm so desolate to trouble the calm of your research like this...I would have liked..."

Jim went on, but Judge was no longer listening, recaptured by his obsessive preoccupation. He knew that the familiar timbre of that voice was slightly modified, and that it was not passion that was lending it those grave sonorities by diminishing its habitual nasal quality. The surprise Jim felt, frightened by finding himself so different from his former self, revealed to him the parallelism of the changes. The metamorphosis was operating in the mental realm as well as the physical. Judge's obscure fear was clarified: one could not manipulate a hu-

140

man being with impunity, like a block of wood, glass or metal.

"Come on, Jim," he said, when his associate fell silent, "it's me who ought to be apologizing to you. I'm an idiot for not having spoken to you sooner..."

He accumulated the words rapidly, desirous of letting his thoughts out.

"As I told you," he went on, "I perceived before you suspected yourself your nascent attachment to our hostess. Nevertheless, I didn't foresee that the inclination in question, in growing, might cause you torments. It seemed to me that it ought to bring about a normal denouement—banal, if one might put it thus—and rather agreeable for you. None of the considerations that you've exposed to me had crossed my mind. I think that they've been dictated to you by your amour, which is combined with a sentiment of a rare delicacy, so I won't permit myself to dispute them.

"As for your resolution to abandon the place before even knowing how that departure would be greeted, that's a different matter. Might you not be causing chagrin to another heart? In addition, by your own admission, your eyes have only opened very recently. The dazzle of that revelation has bowled you over. In those conditions, isn't it imprudent for you—and for another—to leave, when your disturbance hasn't calmed down?

"Frankly, I advise you not to act with so much precipitation. In order not to inspire cruel regrets subsequently, a decision of that gravity needs to be ripened at length."

"Perhaps," hazarded Jim, weakly, sketching a timid smile. In reality, he was not unduly determined to put his heroic resolution into execution immediately. He headed toward t he apparatus, as he had acquired the habit of doing at the beginning of every afternoon.

With a spontaneous movement, Judge stopped him. "Don't y ou t hink," he said, "that a turn in the open air would be preferable for you, after that mental shock?"

He dared not explain to him, and would not, in any case, ha ve been ab le to legitimate c learly to himself the motives for his gesture. Under the empire of an embarrassment analogous to the instinctive recoil that had led him, at the moment of carrying out his first trial, to delay the debut, he had seized Jim's arm in an almost reflexive fashion. It s eemed to him t hat e verything w as a bout to recommence, that there w as a ne w leap into the u nknown to make.

Jim did not perceive his associate's trouble, and did not see anything in his words by an obliging manifestation of an excessive scrupulousness.

"You're f orgetting," he s aid, "that i t's today tha t we'll f ind out w hether t hose pe ople i n t he A rdennes have suc ceeded or not i n their g reat affair. We're approaching the decisive moment, and you must be curious to know the result. For myself, I hope it will be a distraction from my difficulty, and I'll lend myself even more gladly than usual, I assure you, to thinking, feeling, seeing a nd listening…besides w hich, there'll be pl enty of time for us to go for a walk. H ave no f ear! I 'm much calmer now. Really, my confessions, and, above all, your a ffectionate m anner of r eceiving t hem, ha ve soothed me."

XII. Listening

The helmet fitted and the lenses in place, once the connection had been established, this is what Jim Broks felt, saw and heard:

Joseph L *** and Georges V *** were walking on the lawn, the emerald of which the storm had revived, around the calmed waters of the pond, flowery with nenuphars and arums, bearing their white calices aloft. They were heading toward the hothouses, without saying a word.

While his gaze followed the play of the three little butterflies fluttering above a basket of roses, the millionaire was suffering a stabbing pain under the right shoulder-blade, a numbness of the shoulder and the arm on the same side—sensations that Jim perceived clearly in his own body. They obliged him, as they did the owner of the Château de M***, to raise the shoulder, shake the arm and inhale deeply from time to time in order to try to attenuate a disagreeable anguish.

In the central rotunda, a wickerwork table and armchairs awaited. Joseph L*** struck a minuscule gong hidden in the foliage.

When the two comrades were sitting before iced drinks that had just been served to them, Georges V*** lit a cigarette, looked at his friend fixedly, and suddenly declared: "I don't understand."

"What?" asked Joseph L***.

"The door was closed, and besides, I observed when I arrived that the storm had sent the majority of our apparatus crazy. On the other hand, the window of the room where you were standing was wide open. Did you see, when the ball arrived, whether it came through the closed door or penetrated through the open window?"

"No. A gust of wind blew in a squall at the same time as a flash of lightning blinded me, so I closed my eyes instinctively. Then, when I saw the red sphere describe the bizarre evolutions I told you about, to finish up settling under the porcelain shelf, my first impression was that it had come in through the bay. I recall that I thought it was ball lightning."

"Well," said Georges V***, "if the sphere was introduced in that fashion, where did it come from?"

"What?" exclaimed the millionaire. "It's my turn not to understand, for my first impression hasn't persisted. On the contrary! Where did it come from?"

"Evidently!" his comrade articulated, coldly. "In the laboratory, where I was until you called me, I didn't observe any phenomenon of that sort; the stove wasn't open; no light, no vapor, sphere, cone or cylinder was manifest. In consequence, you witnessed an arrival without me having registered a departure. That's what I don't understand."

"According to you, then, we have to admit that the sphere emanated from somewhere else. Where? It's absurd, for it would be necessary to suppose at the same time an extraordinary, implausible coincidence, since it would be by chance that it emitted those vibrations according any matter present to its unique diapason a condition that happened, miraculously, to be precisely the one we wanted to create: gold.

At that moment, Jim could not help crying to Judge: "They've succeeded, Faxton! But I don't know how! Terribly obscure! They know hardly anything to themselves, and are arguing..."

Meanwhile, Joseph L*** continued: "On that point, there's no doubt, is there? So isn't it simpler..."

"...To believe that it escaped from the oven?" interrupted George VI***. "No, for me, who kept my eyes open and saw nothing, that's impossible."

"Suppose, however, radiations that didn't impress any of our senses—they exist—and which were condensed in a visible form subsequently, when I perceived the red sphere?"

"No," repeated his comrade, stubbornly. " I still don't understand. The radiations of which you speak light electric bulbs, and are manifest by actions that reveal them indirectly. You imagine that others might be produced. Why that hypothesis when we possess a fact?"

"Which one?" demanded the owner of the Château de M***. "We possess a collection of them: the evolutions of the sphere...the death of the bee...the music that died away... the transmutation of the table...and I could go on."

"The fact to which I'm alluding," the other relied, "and of which it's necessary to take account, is that the large bay, open to the garden, offered a route of easy access, while, on my side, the doors and windows remained closed, intact."

"You'll recognize that the gold is also a fact..."

Georges V*** stood up, approached his friend, and said: "So you believe that we've succeeded? Answer me frankly."

The millionaire remained pensive.

The engineer went on: "Come on! I know your initial skepticism regarding the manuscript, and that our retouches in order to bring the experiment into conformity with the data of modern science served you primarily as a pastime, a pretext for utilizing resources and spending t he ex cessive i ncome of t oo large a f ortune. You hoped, admit it, to verify the negligibility of all alchemy rather than to succeed in reconstituting the egg and discovering the philosophers' stone.

"For me, it was quite different. I dreamed about a possible s eries of uno rganized s ubstances. I t w ouldn't develop from t he s imple t o t he c omplex, but from t he lighter go the heavier and, unlike the evolution of living matter, it would be reversible, with the consequence that one would be able to go up and down the scale at will."

"I know… but, the gold?"

"The gold, yes. That's a fact, a frightful fact, since it has nearly crushed us with its evidence. Nevertheless, it doesn't provide the proof that you want to take from it. given that, I repeat, as soon as I went into the laboratory I was struck by the malfunctioning of the majority of the apparatus and the complete arrest of some mechanisms. Our experiment was thus severely compromised.

"Under the influence of emotion, back there, to tell the truth, I adm itted the success o f t he C hevalier de Versepleure; I had a clear vision of his success and mine. I t ranslated easily one o f the p assages i n his g rimoire. What do you expect? The analysis that we had just made had bow led me over. Pure gold! That bee, changed before our eyes i nto a m etal i ngot! That w as e nough t o make me crazy. But now, coolly, in spite of my desire not to have labored in vain, it's impossible, on reflection, to find the slightest reasonable c onnection be tween o ur trial, b roken dow n a nd s uspended w ell be fore the production of any phenomenon, and the appearance of the sphere."

"Why, Georges? The perturbation of the apparatus and their arrest might signify that they had finished playing a role?"

"In that case, the gold would have been inside the crucible, already about to cool. Rigorously, the oven itself would have presented traces of the metal or a transformation of one of its parts into gold. I didn't observe anything similar. As for the radiations susceptible, according to your hypothesis, of traversing partitions, walls, doors or windows, they would have been propagated in all directions, in the fashion of other waves spreading out in space. Their ulterior condensation would have provoked the birth of several spheres, not one alone. What do you expect? I don't understand!"

He sat down, drank his orangeade in a single draught, and lit another cigarette.

Joseph L*** replied: "It's necessary not to judge in accordance with the ideas we had an hour ago. You talk about facts. Incline before them, then. Register them! You can try to interpret them afterwards. What has become of your enthusiasm? You mocked my fear of a success, and now..."

"I can't consider that as a success."

"Evidently. We began—without any great hope, I grant you—an enterprise that we thought grandiose, or vain. We didn't suppose it to be terrible. Now, we're in the presence of a result, and you're rebellious because the event was produced in a form that your calculations hadn't foreseen."

"No, old chap! That's not true. I only doubt that the result was due to us. I'm hesitant to admit that our apparatus was responsible for its production."

"Sapristi! If the sphere didn't come from our egg, where did it come from?"

"Through the open bay window."

"From the sky, then! An aerolith? It would have been more likely to come through the roof."

"That's precisely what I don't understand," Georges V*** confirmed. "And I want to understand!"

"Well, let's try. I won't refuse to abandon my hypothesis in favor of yours, if there's a reason to do so. Let's go and see the apparatus again, your door and my window, and let's examine everything seriously. Although I remember perfectly that, to begin with, the sphere described a kind of spiral, and rose toward the bay before falling. An aerolith wouldn't have behaved like that. And that noise, the continuous hum, you heard it too? Then it fell silent. Finally, I don't know of any examples of aeroliths that vanish after having created gold around them. They cool down and remain. Furthermore, they contain, as you know, iron rather than gold.

"At any rate, the examination of the places, to which we can devote ourselves now without danger, might inform us. In addition, it will always be permissible for us to recommence the experiment; within three weeks we'll know what we're dealing with..."

Judge, who was, as usual, observing Jim Broks, saw him go pale then and raise his eyes to look at him. He advanced, while Jim said in a faint voice: "They're talking about recommencing the experiment, but ... oh! I don't know what I'm experiencing... They've fallen silent... Oh! I don't feel very well. Help me, I beg you, to take off the helmet... What's the matter...! Quickly!... I've never had the slightest difficulty before in taking it off... but today..."

He strove in vain to disengage his head.

Surprised, Judge examined it at closer range and perceived that, in fact, a double cushion of flesh was beginning to stand out in relief around the brass crown, indicating that it had suddenly become too tight.

Meanwhile, Jim was breathing with increasing difficulty. His bloodless face was altering rapidly, putting on a horrified mask. After having agitated his lips without any sound emerging from his wide open mouth, his muscles relaxed, his arms fell alongside his inert body, and he ended up collapsing in his friend's arms. Judge laid him on the floor immediately and ran to search for some pincers. At the first stroke he succeeded in ripping the metallic band of the apparatus, which fell.

Nevertheless, Jim's faint was prolonged for a further two or three minutes, which seemed frightfully long to Judge. Finally, a prolonged inhalation swelled Broks' chest. He opened his eyes; a few moments later he had recovered his self-possession completely. He passed his hand over his forehead, which was still striped by a broad red mark, and with Judge's help he stood up, painfully.

Still sustained, he staggered a few paces, which took him as far as a chair, into which he fell rather than sitting down.

There, his strange malaise dissipated gradually. Judge held out a glass of whisky to him. He drank it in small sips, very slowly, while frissons agitated him several times, without his associate being able to tell whether they were caused by the warmth of the alcohol or the memory of some anguishing scene. He dared not interrogate him.

Jim talked of his own accord.

First of all, smiling, he held out his hand toward Judge's, and when he had seized it, he shook it energetically. Then his first words were: "Thank you, Faxton."

As Judge demurred politely, he added: "Really, you saved my life. It was just in time, I assure you, that you wrenched the helmet off, otherwise, at this moment, I'd be exactly as dead as the proprietor of the Château de M***."

"What are you saying, Jim?"

"Very definitely the truth, alas."

A vague cold sweat moistened Judge's temples and palms; this time, he did not protest. He only thought that an absence of a few seconds would have sufficed to render him involuntarily homicidal. Had it extended that far, then, the danger that he had sensed without being able to specify the menace exactly?

He shivered as he represented to himself the imprudence he had committed, ignorant of the peril that there was in unleashing thus, blindly, unmeasured and inexorable forces. The reality drew away ironically from his dreams and devastated them pitilessly.

Sadly Jim repeated: "The truth, Faxton, the truth!"

Then, again, silence fell.

The distant agony, which had nearly struck a life here and extinguished it by its unexpected repercussion, weighed upon the one with all the terror of his recent memory, and put on the shoulders of the other a leaden cape, under which he was curbed, simultaneously feeling pity for the abrupt end of a sympathetic stranger and seized by remorse at the thought that he might have killed Jim.

Outside, the sun animated that northern garden with an orgy of southern colors. Raising his head, Judge was influenced by that joy of the exterior décor, its contrast with his macabre reflections, and he almost criticized himself for having accepted his associate's funereal revelation without reserve. His emotion dissipated and a reaction set in.

He began to argue with himself. In sum, Jim's faint did not necessarily signify that it was linked to a mortal accident that had overtaken the owner of the Château de M***. It might have been due to an excessively abrupt internal transformation, of the kind that had rendered the brass crown too tight.

With that in mind, he asked Jim: "Do you still have a headache?"

"No," he replied. "I only feel very tired. But why are you looking at me like that? And what happened? Why wasn't I able just now to rid myself of an apparatus that I took off so easily before?"

"Hmm!" replied Judge. "Don't tire yourself out any more, my dear friend, by asking such questions. Would you like to go up to your room and rest? I promise you that I'll satisfy your curiosity later."

XIII. Life Goes On...

As soon as he was lying comfortable on a chaise-longue, Jim Broks did not take long to go to sleep, after having asked his friend to wake him up at tea time.

Before that body, tranquilly extended, and that face, on which sleep conferred a serene immobility, permitting a meticulous and prolonged examination. Judge felt gripped by a strange malaise, for it was no longer permissible for him to doubt. Like an adolescent who, emerging from the ingrate age, takes on a virile appearance different from his past form, in spite of his former familiar childish physique still being perceptible, often embellished, through his new mask, Jim appeared to him simultaneously as a stranger and a familiar individual, with whom he had lived for so many hours, but who lacked a habitual element, his ugliness. He could not weary of looking at him, so similar and so different. Although forewarned in a way of that variation by the various remarks he had already made on that subject on previous occasions, he could not get used to it. It left him surprised and emotional.

He ended up shaking his head several times, sighing, and then left silently and went to his own room. There he opened the drawer, locked with a key, of a small writing desk, took out his notebook, and wrote:

When I commenced to relate at length in these pages the succession of our experiments, I scarcely suspected that I would be constrained so quickly to close the list.

I hoped to present an important collection of clear and conclusive observations relative to an exception case of provoked telepathic hallucinations, due, as I had supposed, to the special conformation and resultant permeability of the fine cranium of my collaborator, which permitted the usage of the apparatus described elsewhere. Checking was carried out easily since the subject remained ready to submit to a supplementary enquiry.

My observations differed totally from the accumulation of nurse's tales and mystifications in which second-hand anecdotes were brought together pell-mell, which have been easily controverted, pure fables subsequently recognized as such and other stories of the same kind, in which we are nevertheless asked to believe without a detailed foundation, without the appearance of the two sorts of stories presenting the slightest detail to differentiate them, and without furnishing us any other means than hazard of permitting us to discern erroneous assertions regarding dates, places and persons, affirmations held to be exact until proof of the contrary.

It became evident, therefore, that only the communication we had obtained, at will, in clearly defined conditions, merited the name, wrongly lavished, of telepathic hallucinations.

All that appeared to me to be very simple.

Life is actually more complex, and experimentation reserves surprises in practice. That, in fact, is what has happened.

From now on I know that the living machine, even in a being as advanced as a human, offers resources of flexibility, malleability and inconstancy, the richness and extent of which we are far from suspecting at present. The day will probably come when we will relegate the notions of the fixity and permanence of species, types *and characteristics, pe rhaps e ven sexes, t o t he r ank of ancient myths.*

Here, the variation has b een pr oduced de parting from the center, the modification of cerebral activity en-gendering, but the intermediary of neural trajectories, a correlative change in the secretion of glands, the struc-ture of muscles and bones, the functioning of organs ad vessels. But w hat this un ique ca se informs us cou ld be put to profit in less exceptional conditions of realization. For one w ould dou btless obtain e quivalent r esults by addressing t he pe riphery, proceeding i nversely, as t he physiologist Brown-Séquard t ried t o do no t l ong b efore his de ath s ome y ears ago. Si nce t hen, phy sicians w ho have i mmediately t aken possession of h is m ethod have limited its de velopment a nd restricted its s tudy b y i ts exclusive application to therapeutics...[11]

Judge was not a man to linger over romantic antici-pations a ny more than sentimental r ecrimination. H e murmured: "Hmm! I t hink t hat it w ould be b est no t to publish this journal so soon.

Then, a fter ha ving w ritten br ief c onclusions for his personal s atisfaction, he a dded the da teline: *Ostend, 17 August 1898*.

With a n energetic s troke he unde rlined t hat m en-tion, a nd r eplaced the no tebook in the d rawer, w hich he locked again carefully.

---

[11] The physiologist Charles Brown-Séquard died in 1894. To-ward the end of his life he claimed that "rejuvenation" could be achieved in human males by injections of extracts from the testes of monkeys, which stimulated a g reat deal o f i nterest, flawed research and optimistic practice.

A few minutes later he headed for the Kursaal, which he entered. He sat down on the terrace and asked for a railway timetable as well as a drink.

He quickly took account of the fact that, in spite of the short distance that separated Ostend from the Château de M*** as the crow flies, it would take him almost an entire day to accomplish the journey, As for effecting it that evening, as he had thought at first, that was even less practical; he would have arrived at about three o'clock in the morning at the town nearest to the residence of the two engineers and would only have been able to set forth again too early or too late. Not wanting to leave Jim alone in the present circumstances for two long days, Judge reluctantly renounced his project. He paid the waiter and went down toward the dike.

Almost immediately, he encountered Madame Lansaert, who came toward him.

"Pardon me, Monsieur Judge," she said, "But... I see that you're walking alone. Is your friend ill?"

"Don't worry, Madame; he's merely fatigued, and desired to rest."

"However, he seems very robust at present. He's changed a great deal since his arrival. Then, I confess to you that he didn't make a very good impression on me; his health appeared to me to be so paltry. That's why, on perceiving you, I was afraid of a relapse."

"A relapse? I've never known him to have the slightest indisposition."

"Oh! Truly? Then... he must have been working too hard before taking his vacation, for I feared that he might be ill, very ill."

"And in spite of that, you accepted us as tenants!"

"It's not knowing me very well, Monsieur Judge, to speak thus. On the contrary, I had a secret desire to take you, f or I f oresaw that o ur c limate, s lightly r ude but healthy, our keen air, the sea and my good Rosa's cooking would put your friend back on his feet, and I'm glad to see that he was fortified so quickly."

"Hmm!" sai d Judge, w ho di d not t hink t hat he should disabuse the pretty widow. "Excuse me. And to prove that you don't bear me any grudge, accept to company me as far as the esplanade."

"Gladly."

The t ide w as g oing out . The s hiny ba cks o f the breakers, elongated as t hey e merged from t he w aves, framing t he m oist sand s, were bordered by l acy f oam. With the eb b-tide, fishing boa ts w ere de parting, r egaining the open sea with a scatter of wings, the color of rust and seaweed. A s iren blared. Son the ferry de parted veering north-westwards.

Pointing it out to her companion, Madame Lansaert said: "That's t he Dover m ail-boat r eturning t o y our homeland."

"Have you never been there?"

"No, I only know it via the descriptions of your authors—or, rather, the t ranslations t hat I 've r ead, which date ba ck at l east ha lf a cent ury—so I ha ve di fficulty imagining England as it is at present. I always imagine it furrowed by di ligences and pos t-chaises, inhabited by gentlemen with side-whiskers in court dress, with muslin cravats, wearing riding trousers and long boots, courting vaporous blonde young women dressed in the manner of 1830.

Judge started laughing.

"I assure y ou," he af firmed, "that w e po ssess r ailways on which express trains circulate, that our roads are traveled by more bicycles than mail-coaches, and that we use electric light as well as the telephone."

Engaged in that tone, the conversation continued with animation. Judge feared finding himself alone with his thoughts, one of which, above all—that of the death of the owner of the Château de M***—obsessed him painfully. He was glad of the diversion that the conversation procured him, and he strove to prolong it in order to escape the funereal haunting.

Madame Lansaert, put in confidence, soon spoke about herself and her past. Orphaned almost in the cradle, she had never known her parents. A few months before her birth, her father, an officer in the army, having been unsaddled during a maneuver, had had his skull fractured by hooves of a cavalier's mount, which was galloping directly behind him and had not been able to avoid him. Two years later, her mother was carried off by pneumonia. One of her uncles, appointed as the child's guardian, had taken her in and brought her up. In haste to rid himself of that burden, when she reached the age of seventeen, he had married her to the son of one of his friends, Guillaume Lansaert.

The young man in question had frequented the academies of Montparnasse in Paris to begin with, but an abrupt diminution of his father's fortune, caused by unfortunate speculations on the Bourse, had recalled him to his homeland. Conscious of the insufficiency of his talent, Guillaume had not hesitated to renounce painting in order to establish himself as an art dealer, only taking up his brushes again for projects of decoration. Shortly after his marriage he fell from a scaffold so awkwardly that he had died a few hours later without recovering consciousness.

That sad childhood and tragic series of mournings had not, however, succeeded in upsetting the fine equilibrium and resistance to the crushing effects of pessimism that the healthy and vigorous nature of the pretty widow possessed. Judge, in listening to her confidences, began to understand poor Jim's sentiments better.

Thus when he went upstairs to wake him after returning from the walk, his first concern was to offer him a mirror.

"Hmm!" he said. "Look at yourself carefully, and tell me whether you don't find a few changes in your physiognomy. Everyone here has noticed them. It would be astonishing if you were the only one not to perceive them.

Slightly surprised, Jim Broks pushed away the object that his associate was holding out to him. He passed his hand over his forehead and replied: "I have no need of that mirror, Faxton, to sense that a profound modification has occurred here...."

He caressed his face; his fingers explored its reliefs and flat areas.

"...And there. Is that the reason I nearly died?"

"Partly."

"Ah! at least I need to know that I've become less ugly. Your turn to talk, Faxton."

Judge started to laugh. "My dear friend, don't count on me to respond to you. Interrogate our hostess on that subject...and have confidence!"

A little later, better than words, which are often deceptive, Madame Lansaert's silences, gazes and attitudes had reassured Jim Broks fully, without him having asked the slightest question, and had confirmed to him that he had ceased definitively to be Double-Head. By means of a furtive handshake under the table he expressed his gratitude to Judge, who, glad and more emotional than he wanted to appear, hastened to swallow his second cup of tea, without having any more of Rosa's succulent cake, in order to leave the lovers alone, under the pretext of going to fetch the evening papers.

Always c onscientious, he boug ht a s heet, w hile smiling, from t he f irst y oung vendor w ho pa ssed, a nd took i t dow n to the beach, now e ntirely unc overed, in order t o read it. H e unf olded i t m echanically, a nd w as scanning a f ew co lumns w hen a he adline a ttracted his attention:

FIRE AT THE CHÂTEAU DE M***

V***, 17 A ugust (from our c orrespondent b y t ele-phone). Last night a fire of rare violence entirely de vas-tated t he C hâteau de M***, i n t he F rench Ardennes, a fine s pecimen of e ighteenth-century architecture and known as such to numerous tourists traveling in our pic-turesque region in this season.

For a l ong t ime t he pr operty of t he C omtes de M***, it had been bought a few years ago by Monsieur Joseph L***, who had restored it completely.

By a tragic coincidence, during the afternoon of the sixteenth, t he ne w owner had succumbed t o t he c onse-quences of a h eart disease from which he had been suf-fering for a long time. Vigil over his body was being kept by one of hi s f riends, Monsieur G eorges V ***, and a nun.

At about one o'clock in the morning, Georges V*** retired to his apartment. Half an hour later, the disaster burst f orth. Si ster M adeleine, al erted by a br ight l ight coming from the outbuildings and the ground floor adja-cent to t hem, quit t he mortuary chamber i n or der t o raise the alarm.

Unfortunately, in spite of the promptitude of aid, the staff who came running were unable to save G eorges

V***, whose apartment was above the library, where the fire, finding a f acile a liment, w as r aging. T he s courge was propagated elsewhere with a rapidity such that the body of Joseph L*** similarly remained in the flames.

The firemen...

Judge di d no t r ead a ny m ore. A n e xcessively pr ecise spe ctacle w as evoked for his ey es, blurring t he white i ntervals and the bl ack l ines; he saw onc e ag ain Jim's bl oodless face a s he fainted in his a rms, hi s t emples circled by the fatal crown, and that body lying motionless next to the apparatus, set up with joy, which had almost brought him death.

He crumpled up the paper.

Nearby, c hildren w ere bui lding a sand-castle w ith furious thrusts of spades, punctuated with loud cries and bursts of laughter.

Large horses were bringing r olling cabins toward the waves, where the incoming tide reached the dry sand, in accordance with the appeals of bathers.

In the distance, the sea, gray-green and white, balanced hulls and sails.

Life c ontinued, indifferently, under t he sun, w hich dappled t he s nowy c rests of t he w aves w ith g olden streaks.

Near the dunes, in the small house embalmed by the perfume of roses, Jim Broks and Madame Lansaert were walking in the garden at a slow pace. They were talking in the future tense, constructing their own future tenderly, like a beautiful palace of joy in which their common dreams would dwell henceforth.

ALSO FROM BLACK COAT PRESS

( ) Jean-Marc & Randy Lofficier. The French Fantasy Treasury (Vol. 1) (anthology)

( ) Jean-Marc & Randy Lofficier. The French Fantasy Treasury (Vol. 2) (anthology)

( ) Jean-Marc & Randy Lofficier. The French Fantasy Treasury (Vol. 3) (anthology)

( ) Charles Lomon & P.-B. Gheusi. The Last Days of Atlantis

( ) Marie-Madeleine de Lubert. Princess Camion

( ) Charles Malato. Lost!

( ) Maurice Magre. The Marvelous Story of Claire d'Amour

( ) Maurice Magre. The Call of the Beast

( ) Maurice Magre. Priscilla of Alexandria

( ) Maurice Magre. The Angel of Lust

( ) Maurice Magre. The Mystery of the Tiger

( ) Maurice Magre. The Poison of Goa

( ) Maurice Magre. Lucifer

( ) Maurice Magre. The Blood of Toulouse

( ) Maurice Magre. The Albigensian Treasure

( ) Maurice Magre. Jean de Fodoas

( ) Maurice Magre. Melusine

( ) Maurice Magre. The Brothers of the Virgin Gold

( ) Catulle Mendes. The Little Fays in the Air

( ) Louis-Sébastien Mercier. The Iron Man

( ) Joseph Méry. The Tower of Destiny

( ) Hippolyte Mettais. Paris Before the Deluge

( ) Henriette-Julie de Murat. The Palace of Vengeance

( ) Marie Nizet. Captain Vampire

( ) Charles Nodier. Trilby   The Crumb Fairy

( ) Pierre-Alexis Ponson du Terrail. The Vampire and the Devil's Son

( ) Pierre-Alexis Ponson du Terrail. The Immortal Woman

( ) Pierre-Alexis Ponson du Terrail. The Police Agent

( ) Edgar Quinet. Ahasuerus

( ) Edgar Quinet. The Enchanter Merlin

( ) Restif de la Bretonne. Discovery of the Austral Continent

( ) Restif de la Bretonne. Posthumous Correspondence (Vol. 1)

( ) Restif de la Bretonne. Posthumous Correspondence (Vol. 2)

( ) Restif de la Bretonne. Posthumous Correspondence (Vol. 3)
( ) Restif de la Bretonne. Posthumous Correspondence (all 3
volumes)
( ) Restif de la Bretonne. The Story of the Great Prince
Oribeau (The Fay Ouroucoucou 1)
( ) Restif de la Bretonne. The Four Beauties and the Four
Beasts (The Fay Ouroucoucou 2)
( ) Marie-Anne de Roumier-Robert. The Voyages of Lord Sea-
ton to the Seven Planets
( ) Louis-Claude de Saint-Martin. The Crocodile
( ) Nicolas Segur. The Human Paradise
( ) Nicolas Segur. Penelope's Secret
( ) Pierre de Sélènes. An Unknown World
( ) Brian Stableford. The Queen of the Fays (anthology)
( ) Brian Stableford. Funestine (anthology)
( ) Brian Stableford. The Origin of the Fays (anthology)
( ) Brian Stableford. Tales of Enchantment and Disenchant-
ment (anthology + non-fiction)
( ) Charles-François Tiphaigne de La Roche. Amilec
( ) Simon Tyssot de Patot. The Strange Voyages of Jacques
Massé and Pierre de Mésange
( ) Louis Ulbach. Prince Bonifacio
( ) Willy. Astral Amour

www.ingramcontent.com/pod-product-compliance
Lightning Source LLC
Chambersburg PA
CBHW032149020726
47496CB00003B/791